New Age Apocalypse ©

John Roman's Return

Book three of the New Age Apocalypse Trilogy Series.

By
William Preston Ph.D

The author has copyright for all three books in series.
The Rise of John Roman
John Roman's War

John Roman's Return

Contact author: kingcribholdem@yahoo.com

Acknowledgments

My trilogy, New Age Apocalypse has been a labor of love. But as with all the important events in my, life I had the help and support of many around me. When I returned to college 1999, my first teacher was Ken Jolicoeur. This exceptional man, who would later be the best man at my wedding, taught me to think for myself, academically, and to always write the truth. His encouragement and mentoring was one of the reasons I was able to go from a forty-four year old man with a high-school diploma 1999, to a fifty-six year old man with a Ph.D in 2012. I would like to thank Tammy Bolotow, another generous person, who allowed me to see the world, and reach my academic goals. Without her I would still be walking around with blinders.

Most of all I want to express my love, admiration and respect to my dear wife Dr. Celest Martin. For seventeen years she has poured her love, compassion and encouragement into this needy man-child. Most of all I want to express my love, admiration and respect to my dear wife Dr. Celest Martin. For seventeen years she has poured her love, compassion and encouragement into this needy man-child. Without her expertise, patience and love of language this book would be nowhere as good a read. She is by far the best copy editor in the world. I thank her for her hard work and support in the writing of this trilogy. I have been fortunate to share the last twenty years with her. She is the love of my life and will always be my north star. Without her expertise, patience and love of language this book would be nowhere as good a read. She is by far the best copy editor in the world. She is also the love of my life and will always be my north star.

    William Preston Ph.D.

Preface

In 1972, I entered college for the first time. My, paper chase consisted of playing pool, chasing women and getting drunk, as quickly and as often as I could. What followed my leaving higher education two years later was a life of drink and drugs. I hit bottom on November 14th 1998. With two months sobriety I reentered college at the age of 44. I obtained my undergrad and then took a three year break, when I ran my home repair business: Rent-my-husband. In 2006, I again returned to college and earned my masters and then my Ph.D in 2012. As I write this preface, I have been teaching college writing for fourteen years. It is a career I dreamed about since I was ten years old.

The day after receiving my degree, I swore that after years of reading countless theory and dull torturous tomes I would stick to one of my favorite genres; science fiction. Like many, I was hooked on the sub-genre of zombies. Over the last decade plus, I have read hundreds of apocalypse stories and though there have been many excellent books on the subject, there have always been plot holes which frustrated me. So during the corona virus, on June 1st 2020 at the age of sixty-five, I started writing a, contemporary trilogy. I wanted to write an exciting adventure while filling in plot holes that were always a sticking point for me in other books of this genre. I began writing the, *New Age Apocalypse,* series.

I am very proud of the *New Age Apocalypse* trilogy. Everything in this series has a scientific basis. I write about climate change, which is dramatically affecting the world. A temperature of over one hundred degrees was recorded at the Russian Antarctic this year. After a three hundred year old carcass thawed and released the anthrax virus recently, a herd of one thousand reindeer became infected and had to be put down. The creatures described in the trilogy have their counterparts in nature. Most of the ordinance used is real. The quarantining of people is happening now. This is a tale of adventure, filled with great characters and heroes. It is also a tale that could very well happen in the very near future. So enjoy this exciting piece of *fiction,* and remember, many sci-fi books predictions over the years have become true.

New Age Apocalypse

John Roman's Return

Book Three of the New Age Apocalypse Trilogy

By William Preston Ph.D

Chapters©

Chapter one-------Aftermath

Chapter two------Anaptýsso

Chapter three----Backlash

Chapter four-----True colors

Chapter five-----Operation Showdown

Chapter six------Confrontation

Chapter seven---Peaceful Years

Chapter eight---A New Threat

Chapter nine----New Heroes

Chapter ten------The Search for John Begins

Chapter eleven--Dangerous Times

Chapter twelve—The Search Ends

Chapter Thirteen—John Roman Returns

Chapter Fourteen—The Final Battle

Chapter One

Aftermath

The morning after Chara had wiped out Anu and his Negeltu, John went to see Sheamus.

At Sheamus' bedside in the infirmary, with Cass next to him, John asked, "How are you feeling my friend?"

"Is me son gone?" John and Cass looked at each other.

"Yes, Shea. But he saved us all. Your son gave his life so Humýsso could live. He wanted us to become better. To stop the hate and fighting," John said.

"Ain't that grand. Ya think ta world will erect o' statue in his honor? Or do ya think ta big shots will just be happy he's gone? How about yerself, John? Are ya relieved ya won't have ta be defendin' me boy when ta Nations found out what he was?"

"John loved Chara as much as you, Shea," Cass said.

"Right. Except I would have given me life ta stop him. You helped him, John. Me dear friend helped me son to commit suicide."

"How do you suggest I could have stopped him, Shea? Chara killed three million Morphs in one shot. How was I supposed to stop that? He came to *me* with his plan. It's what *he* wanted, Shea. Not me or Cass or you. It's what *he* wanted. In the end I agreed. So, if it helps your pain to blame me, go ahead, Shea."

'I can handle me own pain. But I need ta go back home," Sheamus said.

"Can he travel, Cass?" John asked.

"Yes. The tranquilizer has worn off. There's nothing wrong with him."

"One of our jets can fly you there," John said.

"No. No. I need ta clear me head. When ta old country calls, it don't want ya ta be takein' ta easy route. I'll make me own way. Goodbye, John," Sheamus sighed.

"Ok. But remember, the only Morphs left are Archieréas,' and the Anaptýsso clan. He and they want nothing but peace. Please don't take out any revenge on them," John warned.

"I'll not be hurtin' anyone who don't hurt me, John. Besides, Chara left no one ta take revenge on, now did he?"

"No. He didn't. I hope you'll come back soon, Shea. You are my brother. I love you."

"Yeah. Ta same."

****

A week after Sheamus left, John and the other inhabitants of the facility emerged to a world that was, as far the eye could see, more moonscape than earth-like. Everything was either flattened or burned beyond recognition. Compared to what it had been, the mountain south of the compound looked like an ant hill. In this alien landscape, John had to convince his people they could rebuild, that the danger from the Morphs was over, and that the future belonged to both humans and Morphs. Over the comms, which could be heard throughout the entire complex, John laid out his plans.

"We have suffered a great deal these last five years. It hasn't been easy to see our family and friends die horribly and turn into things we didn't recognize. But we must think of the future. We can't let the past cloud our thoughts and hearts. Chara saved Humýsso. He was not human. He was an AI." There rose a chorus of voices from the crowd. "Yes. An AI. The thing the world feared so much it destroyed all his kind. He hid for years in the wilderness. If he had been that thing everyone thought AI were, he could have done irreversible damage to humankind. But he didn't. He hid out of his own fear, but when the world needed him, he helped. Helped at the cost of his own life. We humans brag that giving one's life to save another is the highest form of compassion, charity, morality. We claim self sacrifice as one of the attributes which separates us from the animals. Well, Chara was not an animal. He was also not human. Yet, he gave his life willingly, unselfishly, to save us. What would *you* call that?" John asked as he pointed to people in the crowd. "We now must face the challenge of becoming more than revengeful brutes. Archieréas and the Anaptýsso want only peace. In return they will help us reach the stars. If we demand revenge because a loved one was killed in this war, remember that only days ago, over three million Morphs were killed. They loved, cared about their own, mourned for their dead; just like us. The time to heal is now. We have no time to create new wounds, new hate, new fear. Come with me to the future, where love, compassion and respect for the *other* is what defines being human. Now, let's get started by cleaning up this mess and rebuilding a new and better world."

The crowd stood silent for a moment and then began cheering and chanting for John:

"John Roman, John Roman, John Roman."

****

Over the next year, John and the Roman Institute spent billions rebuilding the world. With the backing of friends and associates in the highest echelons of the Nations political elite, John was able to form a tentative peace between humans and what was left of the Morph population. One major point of peace, which exposed just how puritanical some Nations still were, was that the Morphs had to start covering their naked bodies. Many people who were going to have to work with Morphs objected to having to see and work with naked, well-hung Anaptýsso and even asexual beings such as Archieréas.

"How are decent-minded folk supposed to work with these creatures as they parade around in their nakedness. It's immoral," Senator Louisa Fromm stated at the United Global Nations (UGN) Consortium's yearly meeting. At that meeting, it was, Archieréas who extended an olive branch. Through his interpreter, which every high official Morph had by their side, Archieréas spoke.

"I have met with the Anaptýsso and our Archon. As most people know these, are our King, Anax; and Queen, Anassa. They have all agreed to wear clothes, as humans call them. However, these *kaunakes,* will be of our own design. We are also writing our constitution and laws, which we will happily present to this, august body next year. Until then, 'May peace rule your house and love rule your heart.'"

For a while, peace between humans and Anaptýsso, was shaky. Murders were usually attributed to Morphs. However, not a single violent death was ever proven to have been committed at the hands of a Morph. If anything, Morphs were the ones who suffered attacks by mobs and revenge-minded humans. There was no longer a need to kidnap people or hurt women to maintain a healthy Morph population. There was actually a waiting list of humans who wanted to become Morphs and with the Institute's artificial birthing program, no human woman was in danger from the Morphs again.

As the peace moved forward, there were more and more opportunities for Morphs in labor, medicine and space exploration. Studies of the Morph physiology showed they were as hardy as Tardigrades.*

This made the Morph physiology perfect for working in mines such as those where uranium is found. With the help of Morphs, uranium was no longer open-mined. This saved the surrounding areas a great deal of radiation contamination. Because of the Morphs resilience, permanent settlements on the moon and Mars were now possible. Morphs would be sent to these places first. Without the need for elaborate, costly, protections, the Morphs could build permanent housing units for humans.

Morph physiology was also curing disease, aiding in human longevity, in organ transplants, and in a variety of other medical procedures. In turn, humans helped Morphs adopt farming and livestock management. By trading crops for Seally grass and raising small herds of cattle which they were able to mix with Seally grass, the Morphs had plenty to eat. This mutual endeavor led to Morph independence and their entrance into world trade, finance and business opportunities. The Nations also found places for the Morphs to live. The Morphs were given dominion over all the world's Outlands. Unlike humans, they were at home in hostile environments. Deemed uninhabitable for humans, the continent of old Africa, now called Anuli, was a paradise for the Morphs, who thrived in the intense heat.

With this welcomed interaction and interdependence with humans, Morphs started to build a solid culture, and to create laws for governing themselves, laws likes the Nations had. Laws compatible with international codes. Though this integration into the world's population as friends instead of enemies would take years, eventually the Morphs would create a Nation of their own. In 2150, the Anaptýsso would become a Nation, Taka, which meant "Home" in Morph language. In 2155, Taka, became a new seventh Nation, which replaced, Anuli and included all the world's Outlands,. After joining the UGN. However, the road was not easy and there would be many who would see the alliance between Anaptýsso and humans fail. Over the next fifteen years John, Cass and the Lads would continue to fight for Anaptýsso acceptance and peace.

****

*Known colloquially as *water bears* or *moss piglets*, Tardigrades are the most resilient animals every discovered. Individual species are able to survive conditions which would kill humans in seconds. Conditions such as extreme temperatures and air pressures both high and low. They have a resilience to oxygen deprivation, able to create gas which allows them to breathe. They are resistant to dehydration, Tardigrades can lose a third of their weight in water. Their resilience to radiation is remarkable, enabling them to endure over one thousand times the radiation humans can. They can routinely go five years without food. Tardigrades have even survived being in outer-space.

Chapter Two

The Anaptýsso

Six months after the last Morph battle, John and Cass settled down in a log cabin, he built himself. Though John could not have children, because of his rare blood he and Cass were very happy on top of their mountain, in their dream home, which came with a panoramic view of the Pacific ocean and the West Coast Haven facility. The two were still active in ensuring the peace between human and Morph remain stable and productive. John was constantly in touch with Archieréas and the Nations; building bridges of communication.

During this time, the Anaptýsso were putting together their laws and constitution. One particular condition the Morphs had for living and working with humans was to be addressed as Anaptýsso. They now considered the term, "Morph," racist. In the meantime, the Nations were writing their own laws concerning the Anaptýsso and human interactions; e.g., rights and conditions concerning podding and breeding, establishing Anaptýsso territorial rights, borders and international trade, homeland defense and a myriad of other rules and regulations concerning human and Anaptýsso interactions.

These laws helped establish Anaptýsso rights in courts of law and on the international stage.

When it came to defense, the Anaptýsso were banned from sustaining any kind of armed military force. However, each Nation had the responsibility to protect the Anaptýsso who lived in their Outlands from "all threats and danger both in and out of Anaptýsso territory." In the beginning, Taka, which would eventually become the name for all Anaptýsso territories including old Africa, would be defended by a contingency force from all seven nations.

Not long after the Nations and the Anaptýsso began working toward their mutual goals of creating and incorporating the Anaptýsso into the world's stage of Nations, murmurs of discontent and anger began to circulate. At first there were whispers from humans about revenge, unfairness, and preferential treatment. Many felt the Anaptýsso were being given too much attention, benefits and financial support. Some humans claimed their needs were being ignored in favor of a non-human species who had caused so much death and destruction. Scientists, answered those concerns by showing that the Morph virus which created the Anaptýsso did not come with instructions on how to interact with humans. They tried to explain that in the beginning of the Morph virus, newly morphed individuals and later groups of Morphs were acting out of newly-formed instinct. They compared the evolution of the Anaptýsso with that of early humankind.

Many scientists, psychologists and physiologists pointed out that the rapid development of sense-of-self and others was the very reason why the Negeltu and the Anaptýsso became who they were and in fact why there was a civil war among the Morphs. Doctor Sam Walsh of the Roman Institutes division of Anaptýsso studies stated in his address to the annual UGN meeting,

"The evolutionary advancement of the Anaptýsso from first pod to the present is the equivalent of apes evolving into today's humanoid form, not in terms of millions of years but of weeks. Thankfully, for everyone's sake, Anaptýsso and humans concluded this rapid evolution explosion has peaked. Otherwise the Anaptýsso would by now have become so far advanced we would seem to them as nothing more than ants. How and why this phenomenon of evolutionary history happened is one of the reasons we study the Anaptýsso."

Some welcomed this line of scientific inquiry but some were scared to death of it. There was renewed interest in religion, with many practitioners believing Anaptýsso were evil or the work of dark forces. Many believed scientists were delving into areas that only God should control. This idea would grow as the years passed and the Anaptýsso became more integrated with human society.

****

During the next five years, Anaptýsso culture, art and habiliment gradually became assimilated by many humans. The Anaptýsso began to clarify their ideas of life, purpose and *pneuma*, or spirit. This "insight," or what some would, erroneously call, "religion" became known as *Omnishka*, meaning, "*All*." This *belief* that the universe was connected and an everlasting continuum of birth, death and rebirth was at the central core of Omnishka. The Anaptýsso adopted this philosophy into all areas of their life. Their fashion, construction, laws, art and interactions with each other and humans began to reflect their belief system. So strong was the idea of Omnishka, that soon humans were practicing it teachings. The "Esina," which contained the philosophical teachings of Omnishka, was translated into New World and even some old world languages. By the time the Anaptýsso joined the Nations as Taka, over two million humans practiced, Omnishka.

Anaptýsso's kaunakes designs began to appeal to many humans and soon became a fad in the fashion industry. There were three different dress styles the Anaptýsso wore. High Priests went about with a toga like wrap. The front was gray, and held by a pin at the left shoulder. The same shoulder's sleeve went to the wearer's wrist. The toga itself ended at the ankles, with a gray belt around the waist. This left the right arm and shoulder bare, an indication to all that the wearer had nothing to hide.

Royalty also wore a one piece dress-like pullover, with straps over both shoulders, ending at the knees. The front of these pieces were tie-dyed in various, colorful, random psychedelic designs. The Archon believed these designs were inspired by the universe. The bright, various colors and final forms bespoke that the King and Queens were not single-minded, and cared for all Anaptýsso. The Maketes kaunakes, consisted of a two piece outfit. The first part was a white pullover tee-shirt like top, followed by a kilt style bottom. These bottom kilts were bright red but they could be adorned by anything the individual Makete wanted, as long as it wasn't too outrageous. The adornments were mainly for clan names, religious pilgrimages, or recognition of service to the Anaptýsso community. The one unifying design of all Anaptýsso habiliments were that the back of every piece of kaunakes was black and displayed no design or adornment. The reason for this was that since the Anaptýsso communicated with their minds, many ideas and thoughts were open to everyone. For this reason gossip, lies, and disingenuous motives were deemed sacrilege. As the book of "Esina" teaches, the black back of all Anaptýsso's kaunakes meant, "There is nothing behind me but the great emptiness. My thoughts or deeds, everything I think or do, is to one's face."

Anaptýsso housing and construction followed specific rules based upon climate, landscape and their philosophy. Each Outland had one village, or city, depending on the number of Anaptýsso. Taka had three large cities and each of these cities had a High Priest and a King and Queen. From the air, an Anaptýsso city resembled a spiral galaxy. At the center was a large double domed igloo shaped unit. Here the High Priest lived on one side while the king and Queen lived on the other. From there the "arms" of the other housing units spiraled out creating circular like pinwheel tentacles. These domed habitations contained the Makete.

These homes were made from a mixture of adobe and newly discovered strengthening chemicals, a perfect building material for the harsh climates the Anaptýsso lived in. Modest and colored a bright earthy tan, these homes had circular windows, with no screens. Anaptýsso had no chimneys or air conditioning. Because the Anaptýsso could regulate their core temperatures there was no need for heating or cooling technology. The Anaptýsso preferred circular shapes which reflected their belief in the Omnishka basic tenant that all things return to the beginning. Again, the success of the Anaptýsso city design influenced many humans to rebuild the Zone sites, destroyed in the war. They were rebuilt with identical cochlear layouts. Of course since humans did not have the physical stamina the Anaptýsso processed, human housing needed HVAC units. Unfortunately, the rapid pace that Anaptýsso culture and philosophy were being integrated into human society angered many people. It was the age-old fear of the other. Instead of welcoming new ideas and new voices, something which renders societies only stronger and more vibrant, these primal fears began an ugly backlash. This backlash which would have perilous effects for both humans and Anaptýsso.

Chapter Three

Backlash

June 1st 2130 became officially known as "Unification Day." Each year the world would celebrate the end of the war and the peaceful unification of humans and Anaptýsso. For a week, there would be parades, proclamations of unity, and awards of merit given to groups and individuals who contributed to establishing peace and positive co-existence between humans and Anaptýsso. Of course each Nation, including Taka and its Anaptýsso territories, celebrated in a slightly different manner. Humans tended to focus on victory over the Negeltu and the benevolent way they accepted the Anaptýsso. The Anaptýsso focused on their culture and their honorable concurrence with peace. Though minor in outward appearance, these insubstantial contrariety's began to widen.

This dilation of differences became more noticeable on the human side of the partnership. John Roman started to observe more groups who were emphasizing discordance between humans and Anaptýsso society. These differences were consistently becoming focused on what groups were calling, the "dangers and threats to human civilization." At first, these groups seemed to be restricted to a small group of antisocial people. But as the years passed, more and more of the general public were discussing these perilous ideas, so much so that some in the political arena were campaigning on just such referendums.

One such group was called the, "Humans First Patriots" (HFP). Their manifesto stated that "Humans should be seen as, 'First People.'" The HFP refused to call the Anaptýsso by their name, "as deformed or corrupted humans. Not a separate species. Though they claimed to wish no harm to 'non-first peoples,' they fervently believed that Morphs should not be given land, be allowed to make laws, or to morph anyone whether voluntary or not." The HFP basic tenant was to let the Morphs die out naturally. However, even that maleficent view began to be replaced in some anti-Anaptýsso groups, such as the, "Adam Society," with outright genocide. Though many of these groups were unlawful and pushed underground, their influence was starting to be felt in the public square.

Three days before the June 1st 2137th Unification Day holiday was to begin, John was asked to investigate a brutal murder, which many were saying was the work of Morphs. John and Cass, along with Bubba and a crew of forensic scientists from the Roman Institute visited the site of the murder along with local law enforcement.

"Can you tell me who discovered the body, Sheriff Lumus?" John asked.

"Seems a couple of kids, who were gong to explore the Franklin caves, came across this yesterday afternoon. There wasn't much left and they were pretty terrified with what they saw," Lumus answered.

"So none of the body has been removed from the area?" Cass asked.

"No, Ma'am. What you see is what we found."

"Can my team begin their investigation, Sheriff?" John inquired.

"Absolutely, Mr. Roman. It's why we asked for your help. Your Institute has the best people to identify who or what did this. I have a lot of town folk looking to find any Morph they…."

"Sheriff," John interrupted. "They are called Anaptýsso."

"Oh. Yeah. Sorry. Any Anaptýsso and hang them from a tree," Lumus said.

"Well then. I suggest you go back to town and calm your people down and we will get to work. I promise to bring you our findings as quick as possible."

"I thank you, Sir. If there is anything I can do…"

"Like I said, Sheriff. The best help you can give us is to keep the peace. We don't want this violence escalating when we have no idea who's responsible. A bunch of out-of-control vigilantes is only going to ensure more violence and possible deaths," John said.

"I understand Mr. Roman. I'll get right on it. Do you want me to leave any of my deputies with you?"

"No, Sheriff. Thank you. My security team will be sufficient. Besides you may need them yourself if things get out of hand in town."

Lumus put his hand out and shook John's. "I want to thank you again for your help. I might not want to give these Anaptýsso hugs and kisses, but I don't want to see any innocent humans or Anaptýsso blamed for something they didn't do. Most of all I don't want anyone going off half-cocked and taking the law into their own hands." Lumus and his deputies left. With night coming on, John ordered the large LED lights on so they team could work through the night.

As the investigation was underway, John asked Bubba to do a job for him. "Bubba, I want you and Agni to go into town; it's called, Wakefield. I want one of you to come in from the south and one from the north. See what the mood is and if you can pick up any useful information."

"You got it, John. I'll have to stir my little friend out of his meditation, but I'm sure he'll be happy to help."

"Thanks, Bubba. What you find out could be very important. If this murder isn't a one off, we must get ahead of it. Otherwise, this could blow up in our faces."

"I'm already gone, brother."

John turned his attention to Cass. "Do you have any immediate first impressions, dear?"

"Hey, lover," Cass, whispered. "On the job; remember?"

"Humm. Ok." John then raised his voice a little bit. "Tell me Doctor Cass. What are your first impressions?"

"Well, Mr. Roman. At first sight one can AHHHHH," Cass yelled as John pinched her butt cheek hard. Turning she ran after John and the two ended up in his tent. As he turned to face her wrath he wrapped his arms completely around her and kissed her lips until they parted and the both of them savored a long deep kiss. Getting control of the situation, Cass became a little embarrassed and ashamed. "John. You know I love you with all my heart but there is a body out there that's been torn to shreds and probably eatin. This is unprofessional."

"I know. You're right my love. It's just that, we haven't been together for what seems an eternity. I just couldn't control myself." John then sat on the edge of his desk and hung his head.

"What's the matter, dearest?" Cass asked.

"I'm getting tired of being the only one who *everyone* brings their troubles to. We haven't been to our cabin in three weeks."

Cass stroked John's hair. "I know. I know. But destiny or fate has made you that person, John. You can't quit now. There are a lot of people and Anaptýsso who have lost everything and a lot who are hurting. There will come a time for us. I promise. But now we must find out what happened here or things could get worse real fast."

"You're right. You're right. I hate it when I feel sorry for myself. It's the ultimate selfish act."

John gave Cass and quick hug and kiss. "Come on. Let's get to work. But I swear to the heavens when this crisis is over, I'm going to fuck you bowlegged."

"Promises, promises, lover."

****

As John and Cass investigated the site of the murder, Bubba and Agni began their own covert inquest. On a hill overlooking the town of Wakefield Bubba said. "Now look here my little friend. You go in from that end of town and I'll go in from there. Let's meet in an hour at the," Bubba looked at a map of the town on his phone, "Roster Inn. It's damn near dead center of the town. The review says. 'It's the place where everyone goes.'"

"Oh yes. It seems to this humble servant that we would want to go there then. It would not be much use if we went to a place where no wanted to go," Agni said with a smile.

"Alright. You're starting to sound like that Irish knucklehead." Agni started to tear up.

"Hey. I'm sorry little fella, I didn't mean anything by it."

"Agni knows. You are not a bad man, Bubba. It's just that this very humble servant misses him a great deal. So much sometimes, Agni's heart hurts."

Bubba put his hand on Agni's shoulder and said, "I know my friend. I miss him too."

The two then went their separate ways into town. As Bubba and Agni roamed the streets, Bubba could sense an intense bad vibe. Everywhere he looked the streets were filled with young and middle aged men. Though there were a few woman and older people on the streets, the proportions just didn't seem right. Furthermore, the woman and older people themselves seemed agitated and weary. On every corner there were groups of four or five men huddled and talking in hushed insinuating voices interrupted only by aggressive gestures. Whenever Bubba strolled up to one of these groups the talking instantly ceased. Stopping at a couple of stores, Bubba wasn't anymore welcome there. When he attempted to buy a beef jerky stick, he was told the store was closing. After making his way to the Roster Inn, Bubba order a beer and a shot of rye. As soon as his drink arrived he saw Agni enter the bar. Bubba gestured to Agni to come over to him.

Stepping up to the bar, Agni said, "This humble servant does not like the attitude of this town."

"I'm with you there, my friend. These people are one step away from bringing out the torches and pitchforks."

"Why would they want pitchforks and torches? They do not look like they want to do any farming tonight," Agni said.

Bubba chuckled a little and said, "I guess you didn't watch much television in the old country."

"Oh no. This humble servant has never watched the idiot box. I was spending too much time finding food."

"Yeah. I understand. Well, what, getting torches and pitchforks, means in this country is: these people look like they are ready to commit violence on certain individuals and if they have to, they will go looking for those individuals with torches to light the way."

"Oh, and use the pitchforks on such personages they find offensive."

"Yeah, my little friend. Now you got it," Bubba laughed. But then, getting serious he said "And there is the worst part," as he pointed out three of Sheriff Lumus' deputies in among the rabble. "I think we need to go see that sheriff, right now. Come on."

Bubba and Agni left, but as they headed for the Sheriff's office, Bubba noticed several of the men were following them. Then he realized that more than one of the men had weapons. Though he only saw a couple of bats, Bubba knew more deadly weapons could be hidden in among the angry looking group of men. It didn't help that they were all white. Stories of lynchings and murdering of black men filled Bubba's mind. He knew that many angry white crowds over the centuries had settled for a black man to satiate their irateness when they couldn't acquire the person they wanted to hurt.

With the mob right behind them, Bubba and Agni burst into the Sheriff's office. There they found that Lumus and two of his deputies had been locked up in a cell.

"What the hell's going on, Sheriff. You lose control of your men and the town?" Bubba asked.

"Looks that way," Lumus said.

"Is there a way to get you out of those cells? Do you want out? If you don't at least tell me where we can get some weapons. Because there's a mob right behind us."

"Of course I want out. Why do you think that bunch locked us up?"

"Ok. I don't see a key," Bubba said just as the door to the Sheriff's office was nearly shattered.

"Agni, help me move these desks and cabinets against the door."

The two men piled up a good lot of heavy furniture against the door just in time to keep it from being torn off its hinges. "How's the back entrance, Lumus?" Bubba asked.

"No need to worry about that. Heavy steel. We didn't want any prisoners sneaking out the back."

"How am I going to get you three out of there?" Bubba asked.

No problem. Look underneath the desk. There's a button in the corner. Press it."

Agni went under the desk and when he pushed the button a set of keys dropped to the floor.

"Those idiots thought they had all the keys. Open this up and I can show you where I stashed some guns," Lumus said.

"Shit, Sheriff. You don't trust your town folk much do you?" Bubba laughed.

"Let's just say I know my constituents." As Lumus and his deputies ran to the back room where the weapons were hidden, a loud bang could be heard at the front door. Lumus handed Bubba a shotgun. "You know how to use that, son?" Lumus asked Bubba.

"Like it was my right hand," Bubba said. "But what's with this buckshot? You got no slugs?"

"Look...Bubba, right?"

"Yeah. And this is Agni," Bubba said.

"Good to meet you, Agni," Lumus said. "Bubba. Right now, this murder has these people a little off their meds. But they're good people. I don't want to start slaughtering friends and neighbors I have known all my life. Hell, some of those young guys out there, I went to school with their fathers and fought side by side with them in the Morph war. Let me try to calm them down before we go all defcon five on them."

"I get it Sheriff. But I need to call John. Let him know what's going on. I don't want him ambushed out there."

"Use that radio there. It's got plenty of power."

Bubba got on the radio to John and relayed what was happening in town.

"Ok, Bubba. Do you need me to send some of the security people?" John asked.

"I don't know, John. I'd rather you keep them there. Who knows if these people are coming for you? I think we can hold out here for awhile. Have West Coast Haven send special forces by air. They could be here in half an hour. I'm sure we'll be fine until then. It's you and Cass I'm worried about. You guys are in the open. What have you got? Ten men?"

"Yeah. We should be all right. These guys are trained and the best. I'll call in the cavalry. Just hold on my friend. Out."

John went to the site and grabbed Sergeant Gloria Maples. "Sergeant," John whispered. "We may have bad guys coming. Kill these lights and go night vision. Move the two armored vehicles so they are side-by-side and have your men set up a perimeter with the trucks as cover. We'll pile up barriers at the front, back and roofs of the vehicles using the equipment containers. They're made of mega steel. It's thin mega steel but it will stop anything these folks have. Set the lights up facing out. If they come at us we'll turn on the high-beams and blind them for a bit. We' ll go with ear buds so we can maintain radio silence."

"Yes, Sir." As Sergeant Maples began to secure the area. John took Cass and put her in the armored truck. He handed her a Glock 9mm. "Just use it like I taught you," John said as he was about to close the door.

"Whoa. What's this? You're just going to leave me in here while you go get yourself killed?"

"Sweetheart. Please. I beg you. If you want me to get killed, stay out here. I'll be so worried about you I won't stand a chance of getting us out of this jam. Please. Help's coming. No one can get to you in this. I must know you're safe."

Cass looked into John's eyes and knew he was right. "Ok. Lock it up." Before he shut the door John gave Cass a kiss. "Give them hell, my love," Cass said.

****

Back at Sheriff Lumus' office, Lumus started a conversation with the leaders of the mob outside the building. "David. Is that you leading this bunch?" Lumus asked.

"That's right, Sheriff. We want those two guys who were snooping around earlier," David said.

"Now why would you want that, David?" Lumus asked.

"Either they know something about that girl's murder or they did it. They was prowling around all evening, like we was idiots or something. Like we couldn't tell they was outsiders. Bring them out, Sheriff. We just want to talk to them," David yelled, as the rest of the crowd joined him in shouting for Lumus to give them Bubba and Agni. "Bring them out, Lumus, or we're coming in."

"I'm not giving them to you, David, and I assure you if anyone tries to take them, they're going to get hurt," Lumus shouted.

"How you going to do that, Sheriff? We took all your guns," someone in the crowd yelled and laughed.

"That must be you Jerry Sims. Every Saturday night I lock you up in the drunk tank and you spew stupid shit out your pie hole. I guess you do the same when you're sober." Lumus then let go with both barrels of his Ah-Fox side-by-side shotgun. "That's just a sample bonehead. Now get home. We have a whole lot of hurt coming your way, by air, in about ten minutes, I'd say."

As the mob stated to disperse, David yelled. "We won't forget this, Lumus." Turning to Bubba, Lumus said, "He'll forget about it. Tomorrow at the diner he'll be all embarrassed and 'Sorry, Sheriff.'"

"I hope so, Sheriff. But we need to get this murder solved and make sure there are no others. I've seen this kind of mob mentality before. Most times there needs to be an explosion and someone getting hurt before they stop."

After landing two F48 insertion choppers, John's men entered the room and let Bubba and Sheriff Lumus know John and his crew were all right. "We air-dropped twenty of our people and they're escorting everyone into town," Captain Don Gershin said. "Mr. Roman wanted me to tell you, Sheriff, they had some important information for you about the murder."

When John, Cass and the rest of the team pulled up to Lumus' office, John and Cass had a sit down with the Sheriff. "I can tell you several things right now, Sheriff. Just from our preliminary inspection, we know that, one, this was not a wild animal. Two of the victims were not killed at the sire. The body was transferred from where she was killed."

"She!!! you know it was a she?" Lumus asked.

"We're positive Sheriff," Cass said. "The victim was a young woman about twelve to fifteen years old."

"Oh, shit. That's got to be Debra Marks. That's not good on so many levels," Lumus said.

"How do you mean, Sheriff?" John asked.

"Debra is the Mayor's daughter and Larry Marks is one of the most racists motherfuckers in town. He hates Mor...I mean the Anaptýsso. He hates blacks," Lumus said as he looked at Bubba. "He hates Asians. Sorry their...Agni was it?" Lumus stared at everyone embarrassed. "He hates...."

"Yeah, we get it Sheriff," Bubba said.

"Well if he's that racist, how did he get elected?" John asked.

"Oh. It's a small town. Look most of these people are good people. They just fear people and others who don't look like them or whom they don't know. Hell they don't like me that much and I've lived here for twenty years. In their hearts they're not bad folks. It's just that lately things have been tough since the mine owners just hire Anaptýsso now. I get it. That bunch work ten, twelve hours a day and don't break a sweat. The radiation doesn't bother them and they work for less money. But there is a lot of resentment. Marks decided to use that anger and he put on a good show of hiding his true colors. He spewed out just enough hate and greased enough palms that he got elected. Not by much, but he won. This here though. He'll light these people on fire now."

"Well with our current information and all the data we'll have by Monday, you can call a press conference and let the people know the truth," John said.

"What truth is that? She wasn't killed there? She wasn't killed by an animal? How does that help?" Lumus asked.

"You didn't let me finish Sheriff. She wasn't killed by Anaptýsso. There was zero Anaptýsso DNA. The murder scene was staged. She wasn't eaten. The so called 'claw marks' were made with a skinning knife. Her bones were crushed by a heavy rock and pulled apart. When 'Morphs' ate their victims they pulled them apart with their bare hands. There was no Anaptýsso saliva or DNA. In fact the only DNA we found that wasn't the victims was human. Yes, Sheriff. This was intentionally made to look like an attack by the Anaptýsso. But I wouldn't sign up the perpetrators for the Mensa society. This was one sloppy frame-up attempt. Tell your people that when you hold your press conference," Cass said.

"We have to get back to Haven, Sheriff. We'll make our finding official on Monday. I'll send down some of our representatives and scientists to back you up. How about you hold your press conference until noon and then we'll put out a press release at one pm. That sound fair?" John asked.

"Yes. Yes. More than fair. I can't thank you enough Mr…"

"Please, Just John."

"Sure. I can't thank you and your whole team enough, John." The two men shook hands and as John and the rest of his people were leaving, a fat balding man came barging into Sheriff Lumus' office, demanding answers. John looked at everyone and he could tell they were all thinking the same thing, "That's got to be the Mayor."

****

Back at the West Coast Haven facility, John and Cass were analyzing the evidence taken from the murder site.

"As I explained to Lumus," Cass said to John. "this body was murdered and moved to where it was found."

"So the whole thing was staged? Are we sure it's Debra Marks?"

"Yes. Her father, the mayor, gave us her hairbrush. The DNAs is a match."

"Alright then. We need to find out who would want to kill this woman and make it look like the Anaptýsso did it."

"Well, we can rule out her father." Just then Bubba and Agni entered the lab.

"No. I wouldn't do that."

"I agree with, John. Did you see her dad? Creep if you ask me."

"Oh my, dear Bubba. Everyone must remember that man just lost his daughter," Agni said.

Bubba looked a little embarrassed and said, "I hear you, my friend. It's just that the guy made my skin crawl."

"John, guys!" Cass said. "Do you really think this...Larry Marks would brutally kill his own daughter to what? Get people hating the Anaptýsso more?"

"My love. Over the years I have seen brothers, mothers and fathers turn on their own kin. There could be many reasons why this was done. Could be plain old murder and the murderer wanting to throw us off the trail. Could be murder for profit. We need to find out if this girl had any insurance payable on her death. There could be a plethora of reasons why this young lady was killed and the scene staged. So I'm not ruling anyone out."

"We need to look for some answers from the town folk," Bubba said.

"I agree, Bubba. But who? They spotted you and Agni right off. They're not going to talk to strangers."

"How about if I go undercover," Cass asked.

"What!! No. No way. If there is someone who is nuts enough to do this, they won't hesitate to hurt you," John said. Cass looked at Bubba and Agni. "Fellas. Would you excuse me and John for a moment?"

Agni and Bubba looked at each other and knew what that meant. "No problem, Cass. We'll go check on...ahh..." Bubba tried to say.

"Guys!!."

"Yeah. Right. Right. We'll check on something," Bubba said as he and Agni tripped over themselves to leave.

Cass then moved next to John and grabbed his shirt. "Now look, John. When we got married, we wrote our own vows. Mine said for better or worse blah blah blah. But the important part was that I retained my independence. This was going to be no, 'the husband rules the roost' marriage. Remember?"

"Yea.."

"Don't talk," Cass said as she gripped a bunch of John's hair with her other hand. "I understand you are worried for my safety and I appreciate it. But if I decide to do something, we can discus it but it will be my final decision if I do it." Cass then sank her tongue deep into John's mouth and stroked his crotch with her other hand.

"Oh, shit," John moaned.

"Your ahh. Your ahh. Abso..absolutely correct, dear."

"Goood. Now, go lock the door, then come back and take my clothes off, lover."

****

Two days after Cass searched for answers in Wakefield, she returned to John with some interesting clues. Everyone was present for the meeting and started to comment on Cass's attire.

"Is that the outfit you wore?" John asked.

"I love it," Bubba said.

"You would, pervert. That's my wife by the way."

"Hey. She looks good," Bubba replied. Cass had on a clinging, short, midriff top which revealed ample cleavage and a skirt so short that bending over, the slightest, would leave nothing to the imagination. Seeing all the googly eyes, even from, Agni, Cass said,

"Yeah. Let me go change." After returning to the lab, Cass told John and the rest of the group what she had picked up from her Wakefield visit.

"I learned two things which I believe can point us in the right direction. First, you were right, John, Debra had a load of insurance; payable on death. I went directly to Mayor Marks and confronted him as to why he had such a high premium on his daughter. As you can guess, he wasn't too helpful. After he realized I wasn't a hooker."

"Wait!! Wait!! why would he think you were a hooker?" John asked.

"Did you just not see how your wife was dressed?' Bubba said.

"Well, where were you?"

"I was at his house, John. He thought he was going to get in my panties; for a hefty price. I knew once I got him there he would talk. I had a hidden camera recording everything."

"Ohh man. You're going to have to tell me where you hid that camera in that outfit, Cass. I mean, where could you put it?" Bubba laughed. John looked at Bubba with a grimace that could kill. "Bubba. One more."

"Yeah. Yeah. Ok I get it. Just funnin'. Meant no harm. Just never seen that side of… or should I say sides of.. or all of.."

"That's it!!! Outside!!! I'm going to…" Cass grabbed John and said. "Hey. Grow up. I love you and nothing happened. No one touched my holy privates and Bubba was just playing. Besides I wore my disguise in here to show off a little. It's my body John. I'll protect it or show it when I want."

"So if you want to go around naked so every person can see what you look like, that should be ok with me?"

"Well, yeah, caveman. I promised to be faithful to you, John. I'm not covering up what nature gave me so your ego won't be hurt.

Two people who love each other should trust and care about the others feelings. I'm you partner, not your possession."

"Alright. Alright. Fine. I'll live with that. But just remember, it goes both ways," John said.

"Ok. Can we get back to Marks?" Bubba asked.

"Sure. I think, Marks is our prime suspect. I believe he killed, or more likely had his daughter killed, for the money. That fact that he has positioned himself as anti-Anaptýsso is simply a set up to put blame on them and direct any investigation away from him," Cass said.

"Ok. But how are we going to prove it?" John asked.

"That's going to take some thought," Cass responded. "I suggest we do more digging and reevaluate the evidence. There might be something in there that can give us a lead into Marks actions or motives."

****

The next day, as evening was falling, John got an urgent call from Mayor Marks. "Mr. Roman. If you want to know what happened to my daughter, you need to come to the mayor's mansion. Tonight and you need to come alone. I can't have the town's people seeing a procession of security forces and your so-called, scientists parading up my front lawn. I know who the killer is, but I will only tell you face to face."

"Ok, Mayor. How does eight o'clock sound?" John asked.

"That works for me. See you then."

"You hear that, Bubba?"

"Yeah. You know that's a fucking trap?"

"Well, maybe. But he doesn't scare me. I'll have my weapons and the car's GPA will track my position. If there's any shenanigans, I can't handle, send in the cavalry."

"Ok, John. But I wouldn't tell Cass. She may not want you to tell her to stay safe, but I'm sure she wouldn't be too happy about you heading over to Marks' place without backup."

"Then let's just keep this to ourselves," John smiled.

At seven in the evening, John left for Mayor Mark's house. After a half hour on the road, a figure with torn clothes ran out in front of John's car. He barely had time to come to a stop. The figure slammed her arms down on the hood and screamed for help. John was able to see is was a young woman crying and asking for help. He opened his door and looked around the entire area. Not seeing anyone else he grabbed a blanket from the back and walked over to the woman. As John neared her she fell to her knees sobbing and shaking. John wrapped the blanket around her and said,

"Are you ok? Hold on I'll call for a rescue unit."

The girl grabbed John's arm and yelled. "No!!! No!! He'll find out and kill us." John looked at the young woman who stood five foot tall with brown hair and a rotund figure. To John she didn't seem that disheveled. At the same time, he thought he might be acting a little too cautious.

"Who will kill you?" John asked.

"My...My..."The girl tried to say between sobs. "My Dad. I'm Debra Marks."

"What?" John asked, stunned. "What do you mean, his daughter. We have Debra Mark's DNA from a murder scene."

"It wasn't me. My Dad must have given you another girl's DNA. He's got lots of girls. There in that cabin. There. Back in those woods. I escaped. You must help me free them. The men will be back any minute. I ran and they're hunting me. But if they don't get me, they'll go back and kill them all."

"Why?"

"My father wouldn't want any witnesses. He's been using them as sex slaves. Selling them. It's horrible. Then he took out a bunch of insurance on me and said I'd be his best sex slave. That he was going to make money on both ends, and also get the town to attack 'Morphs.' He calls them that racist name even after all these years."

"Alright. Let me call in some hel...."

"No!! We must go now." Debra threw off the blanket and started to run into the woods but John grabbed her. "Let me go!!! I have to help them," Debra yelled.

"Alright. Calm the fuck down. I don't know if you're crazy or your father is this monster you claim he is. But if there are armed men in these woods, you yelling like a fucking nut is just going to alert them we are here. Now calm down and let me get my gear. Then we'll go after these girls you claim are being held captive."

John went back to the his SUV and armed up. He also pushed the red panic button underneath the dash board. Returning to the girl he said. "Alright. Let's go."

****

Back at the Haven Facility, Bubba heard John's alarm. He located the area on his map and told Agni to get Sergeant Maples' rapid force team ready to go. As Bubba was loading the last of the equipment into the armored truck, a call from HQ came over his comms.

"Hey Bubba," Corporal Damon said. "There's a girl at the gate. Says she needs help. She's ranting that her sister and some other girls are being held captive by Mayor Marks. She also says that John is walking into a trap."

"How would she know John's out there?" Bubba asked Agni.

"This humble servant doesn't know. But Agni suggests we ask her."

Bubba met the woman at the gate and as soon as he laid eyes on her something inside him started to glow warm. Though she was a good two feet shorter than Bubba, this tiny, slim, beautiful woman, with almond shaped eyes, silky long black hair and flawless skin, owned Bubba's heart at that second. The young woman wrapped her arms around Bubba as far as she could and said, "Please! Please. You must help my sisters and the others. They are in grave danger."

"Easy," Bubba said as he gently pulled the woman's arms from him. Kneeling down to the woman's eye level, Bubba continued. "First, what's your name?"

"My name is, Kimiko Sato. Please…" She said, fighting tears. "Please help my sisters."

"You said they were being held by Mayor Marks?"

"Yes. Marks and his daughter."

"What?" By now the team was ready to go and Agni said, "Bubba. Talk to the young woman in the truck. We must go."

"Yeah. Yeah. Of course. I don't know what I was thinking." Agni looked at Bubba and the way he was starting at Kimiko. "This humble servant knows what you were thinking."

"Huh? What are you talking about?"

"What do you think, my friend?" Bubba looked at Kimiko and then back at Agni.

"I'd advise you not to say anymore, little fella." Agni just nodded his head.

"Everyone ready?" Bubba shouted as he took the driver's seat in the armored truck. Everyone double tapped the horns of their vehicles and the convoy rolled out.

****

Finally at the cabin, the woman who called herself "Debra Marks" and John entered the old log structure and Debra immediately went to the small kitchen. There she moved a dirty table and picked up a shredded, worn rug. Then she bent down and opened a hatch in the floor. As soon as she did, John looked into the cellar and saw several bound and gagged women. He also felt a sting in the back of his neck. Within seconds, John could feel his legs and arms tingling so he sat down and looked at the person he knew injected him: Debra Marks. No longer agitated or hurt. In fact, she was smiling from ear to ear.

"HAA. HAAA!! Whoa!!! Yes!! Down goes Frazier!! The great John Roman and I got him. Dad!!!" Debra yelled as she jumped up and down, gleefully clapping her hands and shouting. "Dad!! Come on in. He's down." Within a minute, Larry Marks came into the room with two ugly looking goons. Standing a whopping six-six, the two muscle bound meat heads were clearly twins. One of the brutes kicked John in the ribs.

"Ha! See. I told you that stuff would freeze him solid. Didn't budge," one of the ogre like henchman said.

"But can he hear us?" Larry asked.

"Yes, Sir. He can see and hear. He just can't move a muscle."

"Good. Good." Marks bent down within an inch of John's face. "Mr. John Roman. Well. Well." Larry's knees began to hurt as his portliness flared his arthritis. "Burtrum, Ernest. Help me up." The two minions lifted, Marks onto a chair.

"That's better. Now, John. Ugh...may I call you, 'John'? Oh, right, you can't talk. Heee. Hee. So... John it is. I guess... I mean with your genius brain they say you have, you figured out the whole Morph murder thing was *fake news*. If you've read your history, you'll know where that came from. A man I greatly admire said it when he was president. Remember when we use to have presidents? This country was America not Tsalaki. We didn't include that fucked up bunch north of us or that shit hole south of us. We were America. The great. We had presidents, not this 'Chancellor' bullshit of a so called, Nation. He was a master at deception. At winning the hearts and minds of the heartless and stupid. Nearly took over the whole country of old America. Well, I'm going to take over Tsalaki, and then; who knows?"

"Tell him, Dad. Then I want to cut his throat."

"In good time, daughter. In good time," Marks said as he kissed Debra's forehead. Turning back to John he said, "You see. The Morphs are never going to be our friends. They're using us now. This Archieréas fellow and his... Oh what does he call them, Debra?"

"Anaptýsso. Fucking Anaptýsso."

"Ugh..yes. That. They are developing a tight culture, which many humans are disgustingly emulating. They will have control of the moon and eventually Mars. They are learning our science, how things work. Make no mistake. Part of that is learning how our weapons work. When the time is right, they will strike and we will become their food and slaves. There is also the need for revenge, John. These red aberrations killed too many. They killed my wife and son. Debra's mother and brother."

"That's right. Don't worry, Mr. Roman. When humans have conquered these freaks, we'll have nightly red roasts and hangings.

We'll give out prizes for who can come up with the best and longest torture."

"Easy, sweetheart. We'll get to that. You see, we can't stop with the Morphs. We need to eliminate traitors to humanity. People like Sheriff Lumus...like...your wife." Marks chuckled.

"You promised her to us," Ernest said, as he moved toward Marks.

"And I will keep that promise, Ernest," Marks said as he held up his hand, palm out to Ernest's face. Facing John again Larry continued, "You have no idea how many people agree with me John. In the defense sector, politics, corporations, you name it. We have tons of patriots ready to strike when the time is right. That time is soon, John. The money we make from these woman, drugs, illegal firearms and of course, insurance fraud," Marks bragged, as he pointed to Debra. "is going to fund the revolution. We are going to take back the world and wipe these miscreants from the earth."

Marks stood up and looked at Debra. "You want to cut his throat now?"

"Yes, Daddy."

"Well be my good girl and make it clean. Goodbye, John." As Debra moved toward John, Marks suddenly grabbed his neck. Everyone looked at Larry and saw blood gushing from his neck where a blade was sticking out of the front of his throat. Ernest and Burtrum went to help him while Debra screamed loud enough to wake the dead. John rose from his sitting position and smiled, because he recognized the blade currently protruding from the Mayor's throat.

As John stood, Ernest and Burtrum couldn't believe what they were seeing. "You...you shouldn't be able to move," Ernest said, dumbfounded.

"Yeah. Well if you idiots had done any research, you would know I have special blood. This shit doesn't affect me long. I was just letting you fuckheads tell me your plans. Just like in some old hokey movie, where the villain tells the hero everything just before he is killed by said protagonist."

"What's he talkin' about, Ernest?' Burtrum asked.

"Nothing important, brother. Let's kill him.

"Sorry boys. Not your day."

As the two henchmen fumbled to pull their guns, John raised his Colt 45 and put a bullet into each man's head. As the two heavyweights dropped to the floor, shaking the whole cabin, Debra screamed again, rushing toward John with her knife at the ready. Before she could stab him, a set of skinny arms wrapped around her body and threw her to the floor. As Debra wiggled, cursed and screamed, the guy who had tossed her on the floor and was currently trying to tie her up, turned to John and said, "Are ya just gonna' stand there like o' bleedin' monkey and not help me now?"

"Well you look like you have it under control"

"Under contro…" Sheamus let out a scream of his own as Debra's foot caught him in the mouth. "Ach ya little heathen ya.

Enough o' this here gollywogin.'" Sheamus then laid a hard fisted knuckle sandwich into Debra's jaw and she went out.

"Holy mother o' God. A real she-devil that one," Sheamus said, as he stood trying to catch his breath. He and John looked at each other for a moment. Then the two hugged tightly for a good long time. After pulling away, John said, "My God, Shea. It's good to see you."

"Aye, Lad. Same here. Same here."

"Where? What?" John stuttered.

"Ach. Later, bucko. Let's get these poor girls up out o' that there hole and to safety."

At that very moment, Bubba and Agni, along with the special team unit entered the house.

"There ya are. Late as usual," Sheamus smiled.

The two Lads stared at Sheamus until Agni broke the spell. Running over to Sheamus, Agni hugged his friend and said, "Oh how this humble servant will have to thank the Buddha for your return, my dear friend."

"Well, sure Agni, ya can do that. But also thank ta train which had o' hand in gettin' me here," Sheamus said. Bubba kept staring at Sheamus then spoke, "I don't know if I should be happy or not. I'm glad to see you but you...you just took off on us."

Sheamus went up to Bubba and put his hand on the big man's shoulder. "My friend, if ya are truly me friend, then understand I had ta do what me heart needed. If ya can't understand that, then I won't be holdin' it against ya ifin' ya don't want ta be friends no more."

Bubba froze and was silent for a second, as he looked into Sheamus' eyes. He then smiled and bear hugged Sheamus, as he lifted the happy Irishman off his feet. After putting him down and wiping a tear from his face, Bubba said, "I will always be your friend, you skinny Irish fuck. Just give me a heads up next time you want to go on vacation. I have separation issues."

"Please, my sisters, the others," Kimiko pleaded.

"Right. Of course. Well get everyone back to Haven and make sure they're checked over medically and get them some food and clothing," John said.

As the girls were all being loaded in to the trucks, Sheamus asked Bubba.

"I can see ya have o' fancy for that there Kimiko, boyo.'"

Embarrassed Bubba replied, "I don't know what you're talking about. But I can sure see you're back. The first thing you do is start busting my balls."

Sheamus' voice got quiet and he said, "No. No my friend. Ya misunderstand me. I think it tis o' great thing. Ya been looking for love o' long time, bucko. You're well overdo for it. I say, ask here out. Of course not this here moment...with her sisters…"

"I got it!" Bubba said sternly. Then, a second later, Bubba softly replied, "Thanks, Shea. You're right. I fell for Kimiko the second I saw her. But why would someone like her care about an oaf like me? She deserves someone better."

"Give ta young lady time ta settle in, me friend. Remember this. A person can't ask for nothing better then ta have another love them with all their heart."

As the captive girls were being taken to the Haven infirmary, Sheamus and John had a conversation in the truck. "So, tell me what happened? How did you manage to show up like some b-movie cavalry, at just the right time?"

"Well, Laddy buck. I have been here for about two days, now. Just observein' what ta set up was. After all, I've been away fer three years, Johnny boy. If ya were no longer in charge o' things, I could just go back off on me own. Then I heard gossip in ta town about ta murder and this here Mayor. I smelled o' rat I did. So I followed ya and then I caught sight of ta Mayor here followin' yer truck. Hah, hah. Yeah boyo,' I guess it were o' b-movie. There was yer truck bein' followed by ta Mayor's car which were bein' followed by me own lovely car. When ya stopped, ta mayor did also and he and o' couple o' goons got out and started ta circle around in the woods. I followed them and well ta rest is history as they say."

"Holy shit. Well, I'm sure glad you came back Shea. Cass is going to flip when she see you."

"Yeah. So ya two got married did ya?"

"Yes, we did, my friend. She's the best thing that ever happened to me."

"Ya got that right, boyo.'"

"Where did you go, what did you do all these years? I thought you were dead. We never heard a word about you or from you, Shea."

"I just had ta heal this hole inside me, John. I never contacted ya because I didn't know what I was going ta do with meself for o' long time. I traveled ta world. Saw new places, old places. Met new friends, old friends. Almost got married meself once. But ta fates were kind ta me and I dodged that there bullet. A couple o' weeks ago, as I was sitting under ta tree where me Da died, back in ta old country. I thought o' somethin' he said ta me once. A friend o' his was in deep despair and was about ta lose everything.' Ya see, ta poor man's wife o' thirty years had passed and the fella just couldn't bear it. So me Da says, 'Get busy dyin' or get busy livin' either way, do somethin.' I remembered me dear Da's words under that there tree and so I decided, though I loved Chara with all me heart, he would want me ta get back ta livin.' At that very moment I decided ta come back ta the place I was happiest. With you and ta Lads."

"Wow. Well I'm sure glad you did, Shea. Everyone's going to be happy to see you. What happened to your Dad's friend? Did he also take your dad's advice?"

"Well, in a way. Ya see ta dirty *amadan,* went home and blew his bleedin' brains out."

****

As soon as John and the rest of the group pulled in to Haven, Cass spotted Sheamus. Running up to him she jumped into his arms and kissed him on both cheeks.

"There, there, me darlin.' Don't be lettin' yer husband see ya do that, now. He might send me away and I just got here, love," Sheamus said smiling.

"Oh Shea. It's so good to see you. I think John missed you more than he would miss me if I left."

"Oh...now. There be o' big difference there, darlin.' John may have missed me, but if ya lovely self were gone, it would break his heart for sure. If John lost ya, it would be like ta earth lost ta sun. There be nothin' but darkness."

"He doesn't have to worry. I could never leave him. He's the light of *my* life, too," Cass said. "But you come a close second," Cass laughed, as she planted a kiss on each cheek and one on Sheamus' forehead. "So promise you won't go away again."

"Well...love, I can tell ya that, at this here moment, Sheamus O'Keefe has no intention o' goin' anywhere but ta the bleedin' showers, me lass." They both laughed as Cass headed for the infirmary and Sheamus went to clean up.

In all this sea of good karma, with friends reuniting and new love blossoming, Humanities' old malevolent emotions of fear, anger and hate were taking root and starting to grow.

Chapter Four

True Colors

A year later, in Rus, Seally grass production and delivery was being held up. At first, not many noticed. However, in a short time the lack of Seally grass projected dire consequences for the Anaptýsso and human alliance. Meanwhile, at the West Coast Haven facility, a long awaited wedding was taking place, in the middle of the beautiful park created in remembrance of those who fought and died in the Morph wars. Two people stood, a bride and a groom, under the two giant oaks whose branches intermingled and formed an arch. Decorated with an array of colorful flowers, Bubba and Kimiko were holding hands getting ready to take their wedding vows. Next to Bubba was his best man, Agni. Beside, Kimiko were her two sisters. John stood in front of the, bride and groom in a black tuxedo and presided over the event.

"Kimiko Sato. Do you, in front of all these witnesses, take for your husband, Bubba Johnson?" John asked.

"Yes, I do."

"Do you do this out of love and of your own volition?"

"Yes...yes I do."

Turning to a flushed, smiling Bubba, John asked:

"Bubba Johnson. Do you, in front of all these witnesses, take for your wife, Kimiko Sato?"

"Yes. I do."

"Do you do this out of love and of your own volition?"

"Yes, I sure do."

"Kimiko and Bubba, do you both promise to love and cherish your time together? To remain by each other's side through sickness and health? Through poverty and wealth?"

"We do."

"Bubba, please place the ring signifying your bond on Kimiko's finger."

With his hands shaking visibly, Bubba put the sparkling, three carat flawless diamond ring, on Kimiko's finger.

"Kimiko. Will you place the ring which signifies your bond with Bubba on his finger?"

Smiling joyfully, Kimiko took Bubba's finger, nearly the size of her hand, and placed a giant, intricately engraved gold band, on Bubba's finger. The rings were wedding gifts from Cass and John. It was their way of showing affection for Bubba and Kimiko.

"Then by the power invested in me I pronounce you, Kimiko Sato and Bubba Johnson, partners in life. May your union be one of joy and everlasting love."

"The two then smiled at each other, embraced and kissed in a way only those who are just married kiss. It was a kiss of love, hope, union and new beginnings. The couples display of affection was followed by many ahhhs and ohhhs from the attendees. As the newlyweds turned to the crowd, everyone clapped and cheered. Cass and her friends shed some tears, as did Kimiko's sisters and Agni said a prayer to the Buddha. Sheamus then yelled, "Congratulations ta the lovely couple. Now!! let's get shit faced ya heathens."

John shook Bubba's hand, "I very happy for you, my friend. How are you feeling now that you've tied the knot?"

"Kind of like when you slammed that fist of yours into my gut, way back when we had that boxing match. But, thank you, John. It means a lot to both of us to have you here."

"Wouldn't miss it for the world."

At that moment, Sheamus, along with the male entourage, came over and jumped on Bubba's shoulders. "Now, come on ya bloody married man ya. We here blokes got some serious drinkin' ta do."

Bubba looked at Kimiko and she nodded, "Ok. But remember it's my wedding night."

"Oh, Bubba darlin,' tis here will be o' night ta remember; I promise ya." As Sheamus and the rest of the crew dragged Bubba to the bar; John turned to Kimiko.

After hugging her he said. "You and your sisters have been through a lot. I'm sure you'll find unconditional love and safety with Bubba."

"I am sure I will. Thank you, John. Bubba thinks the world of you. We know they wanted you in Rus, but it meant a lot to Bubba that you were here."

"I was honored to be here for both of you." But I do have to get going. Please have a wonderful night and tell everyone I should be back in a week or so."

****

The next morning, as everyone was working off massive hangovers, John was getting dressed. Cass woke up and asked, "Where are you going this early?"

"I have to go to Rus. They seemed to have some issues that need my attention."

"I hope you're not going alone."

"Of course not. I'm taking Sergeant Maples and her team of special opts with me."

"You're not taking any of the Lads?" Cass said, as she let the covers fall off of her naked body.

John stopped dressing and said, "Ahh..no. Bubba just got married, Agni isn't geared for this sort of thing and Sheamus is probably going to be drunk for a few days. Why spoil their fun. It's pretty routine I think. Most likely some workers want more pay or improvement of conditions. There is always a lot of internal greed going on, so maybe some official has been skimming the worker's pay.

Cass then purred like a cat, as she ran her hands over her breasts. Maybe you should come back to bed and think it over some more. John began to undress, saying, "Well...I'm..sure the team and plane are going to need an hour or so to get ready." Jumping back into bed, the two wrestled and made passionate love for the next hour. As Cass slept, John dressed and quietly made his way out of the room. Before he left, he hesitated and went back to Cass. Just after he gave her a soft kiss on her forehead she opened her eyes and said playfully, "What? Did you think I was asleep? Just wanted to see if you would kiss me before you left." Cass grabbed, John's shirt and pulled his lips to hers. After a long embrace she whispered, "Take care of yourself. Please."

****

Gathering some last minute things from his office, John heard a knock on their door.

"Come in."

Agni entered the room and said, "Hello, John. If you have a minute, this humble servant would like to talk to you."

"Of course, Agni. What can I do for you?"

"I need to go back to my village in, Acharya. Agni's mother is very sick, very sick."

"Damn, Agni. Let me get the med-transport out and we'll get you, and the best medical care we have, in a couple of hours. I'm sure we can help her."

"Oh thank you, dear friend. But no. Agni's, dear mother would not want that. She is a firm believer in the great Buddha. She would not want anything to be in the way of her reunification with the universe. When it is our time, we gladly meet our ethereal Buddha. All this humble servant selfishly desires is to kiss her one last time and say goodbye."

John put his hands on Agni's shoulders and said, "Of course, Agni. Anything you need. It's at your disposal. Did you want any of us to go with you?"

"Oh, thank you, but no. This visit is very personal. It is a family only tradition," Agni looked up at John and stuttered, "Not...not...that you and the others are not fam...Agni...means...it...is traditional....and this."

"Agni. Stop. It's ok. I understand. Go back and see your mother. We will be with you in spirit. Stay as long as you need."

"Oh, this humble servant will be back within a week, John. Right after we burn her body and spread the ashes on the waters of the Ganges."

"So you think she will be dead in a week?"

"Oh, this humble servant doubts that. Agni will be lucky to get there in time before she passes. It's just that when a matriarch such as Gaurika Arya ascends to glory, the family has a week long party. There is food, drink, dancing and many pretty young women looking for husbands."

John's face took on a puzzled look. "Hold on, Agni. I thought you didn't drink or dance?"

"Oh, yes!! Normally, this humble servant does not indulge in such wanton, lascivious, and

Bacchanalian conduct. But on such an illustrious occasion as this, it would be a mortal sin not to."

Trying not to laugh, John said, "Well...by all means take the fastest jet we have and I hope everything works out." Agni smiled and hugged John.

"Agni thanks you so much for understanding, my dear friend. Would you like this humble servant to bring you some of Gaurika Arya's ashes?"

"No! I..mean. I'm sure it would be better that all her ashes are spread over the Ganges," John assured Agni without laughing.

"Then, Agni will see you in a week, my friend."

****

Before leaving for Rus, John had to stop by and see Archieréas. Along with help from the Roman Institute's engineering and design division, was putting the finishing touches on the Anaptýsso's, first, officially recognized city, Principium.

Arriving at Principium, John was immediately impressed by the look and layout of the city. He also noticed that flying next to the Tsalaki flag was a flag he didn't recognize. He assumed it was the new flag of the Anaptýsso. The flag was a solid maroon color with a symbol in the middle that John didn't recognize. "Wow. I've been out touch. I need to have a long talk with Archieréas," John thought to himself. At that moment he saw a greeting committee coming toward him with Archieréas in the lead.

As the group and Archieréas walked up to John, they all bowed. As they did, they simultaneously held their left hand palm up and swept their right arm across the front off their body. John did nothing, fearing to repeat the act, not knowing if it would be an insult or not.

Archieréas was the first to think. "Hello my dear friend. It has been far too long since we have seen each other."

"Yes. Yes," John thought as he gave Archieréas a quick hug. "Is that the Anaptýsso's new way of greeting?"

"Yes it is. The bow is of course for respect, the hand out with palm up, is to show the greeter has nothing to hide and the sweeping of the right hand symbolizes that any negative feelings are swept from this meeting. Unfortunately, some Anaptýsso use it as a means of power display. How low one bows is beginning to creep into the greeting. The same can be seen in Asian cultures."

"Yeah. Well maybe you don't want to blend in with humans so much you lose what it means to be Anaptýsso."

"I quite agree, my friend. Come let me show you our city and we can talk at my home."

"Let me ask you. I saw, at the front gate, what I assume is the national flag of the Anaptýsso. The maroon flag with a symbol I don't recognize."

"Yes. It is our flag. What do you think the symbol means, John?"

"Well. It kind of looked like a snake eating its tail. Intertwined through the center of the circle is what looks to me like a lemniscate."

"I would say that is a pretty good interpretation of the symbol, John. Though the circle is not a snake. It may look like your symbols of a snake eating itself but our ideogram is meant to illustrate rebirth and time. The infinity design intertwining the circle represents that birth, death, and rebirth have an infinite connection throughout the universe."

"Gee. That's some heavy shit for a flag. Sure beats those tricolor pieces of shit countries use to fly."

As the two friends made their way to of Principium, John couldn't help admiring the luscious hanging gardens and tree-lined lanes. The whole city was spotless. Anaptýsso could be seen holding hands and there were even humans shopping and strolling the grounds of the city.

"This place is amazing, Archieréas. I saw the blueprints and models but seeing it in real time and finished is truly remarkable."

"Thank you, John. The Roman Institute's help has been invaluable. This design works for every temperature and terrain the Anaptýsso inhabit. We also want to thank you for not only helping us, but more importantly, *teaching* us. Many humans we work with are happy to do things for us in exchange for capital, but not many will teach us. For any society to move forward, they must be able to do for themselves. If we are dependent on humans for everything, are we not slaves?"

"I quite agree. If someone had told me ten years ago, I would be standing in an Anaptýsso city which contains so much beauty, with humans working and living along side Anaptýsso in peaceful coexistence, I would have said they were crazy. But look, here it is and just seven years after the war. Humans and Anaptýsso together peacefully in a city the Anaptýsso designed and built. It's just wondrous, Archieréas. When we get to your home I have a ton of questions. One is this: why are so many Anaptýsso holding hands and looking very affectionately at each other?"

"Yes, John. I'm sure you have questions. We have been developing rapidly, on a cultural level. Not like the evolutionary one your scientists said we did when we first morphed. You have been busy with so many of the world's problems, you may have fallen behind on the progress the Anaptýsso have made. Did you know I have been elected, not appointed but elected, to serve on the Tsalaki council?"

"No. No, the last I heard was your appointment to the council as an ambassador for the Anaptýsso. I knew your name was on the ballot this election, I voted for you, but to be honest I thought it a long shot. I haven't heard the results yet. So you're telling me you won?"

"Yes, indeed, John. By a large margin in fact."

"That's fantastic, Archieréas, hopefully more Anaptýsso will be elected to local positions also."

As they neared the center of the city, John saw three large domed buildings positioned in the middle of the city square.

Separate but connected in the middle, the three houses were home to the Anaptýsso, Anax and Anassa. The third building was home to Archieréas. When John entered he was amazed at the colors and art work hanging from Archieréas' walls. The lighting gave a consistent ambiance to the rooms. Plush couches with lush pillows made one think that if they sat down they would simply sink into a warm embrace. The entire home was a display of modern efficiency with clean lines and exquisite beauty everywhere one looked.

"This place is gorgeous, Archieréas. How much of this is your idea?"

"I would say sixty to seventy percent. The designer, Cheryl Lansing, aided me a great deal with bringing my ideas to fruition. She also knew exactly what materials were needed for the concept."

"I am very happy for you and the Anaptýsso, Archieréas. This goes far beyond anything I could have hoped for after such a brutal war. I thought this kind of thing would take decades to accomplish; if possible at all."

"I understand, John. We have worked very hard and made great sacrifices to keep the peace and be accepted into society." As the two sat, Archieréas called for drinks. A Makete entered with a tray of food and drinks. John looked a little bit worried but Archieréas assured him.

"Don't worry, John. It's not human flesh or blood based drinks. We have Makete from around the world who have made cooking Seally grass a specialty. Many of our recipes and dish creations are now being sold to humans. It's a big part of our GNP.

The low caloric and high protein is favored by many humans. Especially since the artistic genius of our Anaptýsso chefs have created dishes whose exotic tastes cannot be duplicated using human food. The drinks are Seally based also. You will get a high but without the hangover."

John tried a bite of the food and his eyes instantly lit up. He then sipped some from his drink and was again amazed. "Holy shit, Archieréas, this is fantastic. I've never tasted or drank anything like this. The flavors are like nothing I have ever had. I can't put my finger on it. It's...like...the taste touches my tongue and just as I get a...um sensation, the taste changes to a different savory flavor. It's as if my mouth is on a roller-coaster of wonderful flavors."

"Thank you, John." Sipping from his drink again and then lying back into the couch, John thought,"

"Now, what's up with a Makete doing butler work and holding hands? I know you all have begun to wear clothes, and I understand that even your fashion is being copied by a lot of humans, but I never thought the Makete were into same sex relationships."

"Well, John," Archieréas laughed. "Times have changed and so have we. Remember many of those who morphed were female. As you know we have a waiting list of humans who want to morph. Since we keep our population at a controlled number, many humans will never get the opportunity. Unfortunately, there are also many human women who want to have sex with a Makete even knowing it would mean their death. Of course we can't let that happin, so the Makete have adjusted."

"But what about you and the Archon? Don't you have any interest in sex?"

"Well. To begin with, John, sex doesn't mean the same to humans as it does to the Anaptýsso. Just as king or high priest doesn't mean the same. We use those terms because it's the closest we can come to explaining an idea or concept from our language to yours. But those concepts are not always exactly what humans take them to mean. For instance, the term King or Queen, means supreme ruler in your language. Just look to your middle ages and see how much power human kings and queens had. But for us, the Archon are more like figure heads. Each society needs someone they can look to for answers, help, guidance. Our Archon serve that purpose. The Archon only have sex to procreate a 'High priest,' like me. Since there are only one set of Archon and one High priest for every Anaptýsso community, the Archon don't require sex after a High priest is born. High priests such as myself don't have the equipment or desire for such things. My title is not about spirits and gods. I am simply an 'advisor' to the Archon and Anaptýsso. Sort of a middle man, in human vernacular. There has to be someone to interpret, understand the Anaptýsso's, desires, needs and bring those to the Archon."

"Ok. I get all that but what about the Makete? They were warriors, now they're butlers and gay, not that there is anything wrong with that."

"Sure, John. They were and are warriors but they have learned to adapt. Become civilized, one might say. Look at many human traditions. There are people who annually dress as their ancestors did and put on costumes and hold parades. But they take them off when the celebrations are over. The Makete have adapted. Isn't that the sign of a true warrior? They have become artists, engineers, chefs, farmers, politicians and they love. Love is love, John. All Anaptýsso know this. We do not differentiate between male and female love. To us, love is love. If two beings care for each other it doesn't matter what's between their legs. I have conducted many Makete union ceremonies. Let me tell you, John. As fierce and courageous as the Makete were in battle they are equally committed in there unions."

"Wow. I need to visit more often. I am ecstatic about how well the Anaptýsso and you, my friend, are doing. But I must ask you: have you heard anything about this Seally grass holdup in Rus?"

"Some, John. Some," Archieréas thought. "Remember, John. We have no settlement within a three hundred mile radius of anywhere Seally grass is grown. It's the one environment where Anaptýsso cannot survive. So my knowledge of what's happening is limited. Are you going there?"

"Yes. In fact my plane is ready. I just wanted to stop here and ask you if you knew anything."

"All I know is it isn't us. Whoever is stopping the flow of Seally grass, the Anaptýsso have nothing to do with it. John, before you go I must tell you that we have been hearing rumors. As of now they are just rumors, feelings. But something is ready to happen."

"Do you have any evidence of someone, or a group ready to commit violence?"

"Nothing I can put my finger on. It's just rumors. The Anaptýsso tell me they are being treated differently by some humans. Nothing overt, just slights you might say."

"Couldn't you chalk that up to paranoia?"

"Maybe. But I have felt it. At the Nations Council, in the hallways. Some humans seem as if they're keeping a secret. They way they look at me. A sort of fake mask, covering fake smiles hiding what's underneath. And what's underneath is a face saying, 'Just wait. You're going to get yours.'"

"Damn. I don't know what to say, Archieréas. I'll have my people dig deep. If there is something there, we'll find it. In the meantime, maybe you should have body guards."

"Oh I do, my friend. The minute we won the seat on the Council a team of five of the toughest Makete were assigned to me." John looked at his watch and stood. "I must go, my friend. Stay safe and I'll see you when I get back."

Archieréas stood and went to shake John's hand but instead, John bowed deeply while extending his left hand palm up and swiping the ground before him with his right. Archieréas smiled and did the same.

****

Five hours after leaving Archieréas, John landed at the Rus airport. "Sergeant Maples. We have an office right by the airport's main building. Secure it. Make sure our people are all right and I'll be there shortly."

"Yes Sir," Maples replied. Then turning to her troops, "Alright move it. Secure the perimeter." As the special teams disembarked, John caught sight of an old friend. As he walked over to the group of people they all started to shout, "John Roman, *nash brat*, John Roman, *nash brat*." A middle-aged man with scars covering a good physique walked up to John and bear-hugged him. He then kissed John on both cheeks and said, "*Moy Brat*. How are you, John?"

"Good. Good, Max. My god; I can't believe you survived that beating Dimitri gave you."

"Ach. Man was pussy. Grand-kids hit harder than him. How you been my friend?"

"Well, since I saw you last, the world fought a war, I got married, lost some friends, you know same old shit."

"Da!!! Da!!" Max yelled as he punched John in the chest. "Come. Come. I want you meet my family." Max dragged John over to the people who were piled in trucks, astride horses and motorcycles. There were men, woman and children. Everyone was dressed as if they had dived into a second-hand clothing shop container at night and put on whatever they grabbed. Some had shoes which didn't match, some had pants that were too big while others had shirts which were clearly too small. They all were decorated with tattoos, earrings, whether they were men or woman, and most had on hats that no one seemed to wear correctly. They looked like characters from the land of misfit toys, except for the fact that they were all heavily armed.

"Everyone, this is man who save patriarch's life." The crowd of people stood mute. "You know, man who keep you clothed and fed." Still no response from the people. Max now shouted louder, "Who protect you from bad people?" Max was pissed at this point and fired a full magazine from his rifle into the air. "Me!!!" Everyone started to yell and shout. Holding their weapons in the air and yelling, "Nash brat, John Roman, *nash spasitel'* Max Devin." After several minutes of this, Max waved his arms in gesture that quieted the crowd. Max then told a man standing next to him, *"poluchit' podarok."* The man ran off behind a truck. "Max, I don't need a present. I need to talk to you about…"

"Da, da. We talk. I forget you know Russian. You are remarkable man, John."

When the man returned with a big wooden crate, Max said, "This is Gregory, one of my six brothers. He was there at the jail that day. Good thing you help Max escape. My family would have killed all of you."

"*Priyatno poznakomit'sya*, Gregory," John said as he shook hands.

"See. I told you he speaks Russian." Opening the crate, Max pulled out bottle after bottle of true homemade Russian vodka.

Handing a bottle to John and then passing out the rest to his family, Max opened his, lifted it into the air and toasted, *"Moyemu bratu."* The crowd all raised their bottles and shouted, *"Nashemu bratu."*

John stood, smiled and lifting his bottled yelled, "Yes!!! We are brothers. *Nam navsegda."*

Then putting the vodka bottle to his lips he lifted it straight up and started to drink. Everyone followed suit.

That night, at Max's estate, his family and friends roasted a whole cow and pig on an open spit. There was every imaginable side dish one could want. Russian folk music and dancing never stopped all night. Occasionally, a woman would come up to John and try to proposition him, but he always politely declined. At one point, whispers could be heard about John's sexual preference. After one of the most beautiful woman at the party asked John if he wanted to enjoy her *manda,* and John again politely declined, Max asked him outright.

"Ahhh. John. You know we brothers, forever. You can tell, Max. If you like men I can find..."

"No, Max. I told you I was married. I love my wife dearly. Her name is Cass." John then showed Max a picture of Cass. "Wow. She is beauty. But she over there, right? When cat's away."

"Look, Max. Whatever suits you is fine with me. Call me old-fashioned but I could never cheat on Cass. I simply would never forgive myself. I love her with all my heart. Cass isn't someone I can put away for a moment and indulge in my base impulses. I know it would break my heart if she lay with anyone else, so how could I do that to her?"

Max stepped back for a moment. "Da. I understand. Was same with my mother and father. It's good thing you have that, John. Not many ever get that." Max then stepped up on a table and shot a few rounds into the air. "Listen, everyone. My friend is not, *gey*. He have wife, Cass. They very much *Vlyubilsya*. So, no more tempting my friend. If you girls horny, come tempt, Max. I ready willing and able."

At one in the morning John told Max that he had to leave. But first he needed a favor.

"Max. I'm sure you know why I'm here. I need you to help me find out what's gong on. Who and why are the Seally shipments being held up?"

"You're right my friend. Nothing goes on around here I don't know. But in this case I am going to have to look further. This not going to be easy, John."

"Why's that?"

"Ahh. To tell you truth, John. When I heard about Seally, I let it be known I wanted cut of the action. I was told by very powerful people, the only people I afraid of, to back off or family would go missing."

"Shit," John whispered. "Look if you need more money I...."

"No. Please my friend. I owe you. Max Devin never forget debt. I owe you life. I find out. Fuck those big shots. They try to hurt family, they have to deal with me."

"Thank you, my friend. Watch your back."

"Da. Watch yours too."

****

The next morning John had Sergeant Maples commandeer the Seally grass shipments. She reported back to John that all the Seally grass which had been processed for delivery was gone. She brought the people responsible for production and transportation to John's office.

"Sir, this is Viktor Evanoff and Sacha Kotov. They are the administrators responsible for Seally grass production in this sector.

"Please sit down, gentlemen," John said.

"Please, Sir. We have nothing to do with Seally grass being held up. We do everything we supposed to," Evanoff pleaded.

"Well, that can't be true Mr Evanoff, or I wouldn't have to be here."

"Why we even here? This is Rus. You have no jurisdiction here. You are Tsalaki. We don't have to stay here. This is kidnapping," Kotov shouted.

"I'm afraid you're wrong there, Sacha. You see all Seally grass areas of production and anything within a ten mile radius of such production is Roman Institute property. You're standing on sovereign Roman soil. You're subject to our laws. We can do to you what we see fit."

"This is lie. I am Rus citizen," Kotov yelled. One of Sergeant Maples men shoved Kotov into a chair. John then pulled out the paper work Kotov had signed in order to be able to work for the Roman Institute.

"Ever wonder why our pay and benefits are so good, Kotov? We only want the best. We do careful background checks but every so often someone like you slips through. That's why anyone who works for us signs this contract. Like you did. It states that once a person comes to work for us they must abide and are under obligation to follow our laws. In short, when you're on the job, Kotov, you're a Tsalaki citizen." John pushed the contract toward, Kotov. "That is your signature, right?"

Kotov looked at the contract and then started sweating and nervously rubbing his face.

"Fuck you," He shouted as he stood to leave. Another soldier pushed him down in his chair.

"If he moves out of that chair again, you have my permission to give him a 138, soldier," John ordered. Kotov looked at the man behind him and then at Maples and finally at John. "Wha...what is.. what is 138?"

"You don't want to know, Sacha." Turning his attention to Evanoff, John said, "Well Mr. Evanoff, do you want to see your contract?" Very coolly he said, "I am well aware of what it states."

"Good. So, I ask you again, where is the Seally grass?"

"I don't know," Evanoff replied.

"Very well, Corporal Jensen, take two men and Mr. Evanoff outside and shoot him." Evanoff laughed.

"You think this is funny?" John asked.

Evanoff looked at Maples and back at John. "Nyet. This is joke."

"Corporal. Do as I commanded, now."

Jensen hesitated and Sergeant Maples said, "Shall I take the prisoner, Sir"

"No, Sergeant. I ordered Corporal Jensen to do it."

Jensen nodded for two of the men to grab Evanoff and take him outside. As he struggled, Evanoff shouted, "You can't do this. This is murder. No!! No!!" Evanoff was straining against the men so much that Corporal Jensen had to smash the butt of his weapon into Viktor's gut.

Kotov was squirming in his seat and looking at John and Maples. After a few minutes of intense staring by Kotov, gunfire erupted from the courtyard. Everyone froze but John.

Kotov yelled, "You said it would be alright," As he stared at Maples. "You said you take care of him," as he pointed to John. "I not die for your..."

Maples gave a nod to the other two soldiers in the room and they went for their weapons. What none of them knew was that John was well aware of Maples' treasonous motives. He had armed himself with a tranquilizer gun and a set of brass knuckles. Before the men could get their rifles up John had put a dart in each one of them and one in Kotov. At the same time he leapt from his seat and with the help of his brass knuckles planted a haymaker into Maples' face. The punch was so hard it knock out most of Maple's teeth and broke her jaw in two places. She was out cold before hitting the floor.

Corporal Jensen and his two men came into the room carrying a cuffed and muffled Evanoff.

"Looks like you don't need our help, Sir."

"No. Her kind usually go down easy. Put all of them in the jail. Make sure you double check for hidden weapons. I want a team of three personnel guarding those cells at all items. Good work Major Jensen," John said. "It's going to take some time for me to remember you're a Major."

"Yes, Sir. Well. it's this baby face which got me the assignment, after all. Everyone thinks I'm twenty instead of thirty-eight."

John shook Jensen's hand and said, "I know this undercover assignment has been hard on you and your family. A year and a half undercover is a long time. But after we're done here I'll put you in for a nice long holiday; on me."

"Thank you, Sir," Jensen said, a little bashfully. "Ugh...the backup transport arrived last night and I have placed our people in the appropriate areas. But we found someone else you might want to see, Sir."

Three of Major Jensen's men brought in a half awake, mumbling, Sheamus and set him on a chair in John's office.

"Where did he come from. He looks drunk as fuck," John asked.

"Yes, Sir. Our own little stowaway."

"I'll take care of him, Major. You're dismissed."

John went over to Sheamus and tapped him on his cheeks.

"Hey, Shea. You in there?" Sheamus slapped the hands that were disturbing his hangover and mumbled.

"Ahhugh...Get yer bloody hands off o' me yer bleedin' feb* wanker, ya." At which point, Sheamus quickly feel asleep. John smiled, grabbed a coat and laid it over Sheamus.

"Sleep, you crazy Irishman."

*Fucking English bastard.

****

The next morning, Sheamus opened his eyes slowly and tried to focus on the man sitting in front of him. Blinking the crud from his eyes while shielding them from the sunlight peeking through the window Sheamus muttered, "Is...that...John these worthless eyes be seein'?"

"Yeah, it's me. What's the matter? Can't handle the liquor at your age?"

As Sheamus struggled to get out of the chair he laughed. "Agh. Fuck yer soul ya heathin' bastard. Sheamus O'Keefe can still drink any man under ta table."

"Sure, ok. But tell me, how and why are you here?"

"So, it were too late ta hop on yer little airplane there so I jumped inta one that was ta follow ya. I hid in ta hold with all ta ordinance and shit. Twas so fuckin' cold I started ta drink and killed both bottles of me Baileys, with o' few chasers from me flask."

"Ok. But why did you feel the need to jump on the backup plane?"

"Ahha, well. I heard some scuttlebutt during ta weddin' that ya was goin' on some secret mission ta Rus."

"Fuck. Couldn't have been too secret if you heard it at the wedding."

"Yeah, true. But I have o' way with getting' people ta talk."

Suddenly, Major Jensen entered. "Sorry, Sir. You have an urgent call from Max Devin." Jensen handed the phone to John and on the other end John could hear firearms discharging.

"Hello. Max. Is that you? What's happening?"

"John. John!! Please come quick. Sergeant Maples and about twenty troops attacking us. They ambush us this morning. Said they here on your orders and started shooting people. We holded up in my house, but they setting explosives. Please, John hurry." The phone went dead

"What's ta matter, John?"

"It was Max. He said he was being attacked by a group of armed men led by Sergeant Maples."

"Maples? I thought she were in ta hoosegow.?"

"Major. Could you go check and see if Maples has somehow fled." Jensen left the two men and John got up. "You able to fight if we need to?" John asked Sheamus.

"Ach, John. Don't be insultin' me now. I've been o' lot more drunk and hungover than tis here and never dodge o' fight over it now." As the two men geared up, Jensen came in and reported to John. "Sir. Sergeant Maples is still in her cell. She's bandaged up but out like a light."

"There, ya see. Maybe, ole Maxy boy has lost his touch more than me, hey boyo'?"

"We'll see. Major make sure everything is buttoned up solid here. Don't let anyone in or out. If they claim they're sent by me, just tell them to wait. Understand?"

"Yes, Sir."

****

Less than a half hour after John, Sheamus and a team of ten left John's office. They neared Max's homestead encampment. About a hundred yards from the site, John could see several smoke trails rising from the camp. "You smell that, Shea?"

"Aye. Nothin' like that there smell, John. Tis the smell o' death it is."

"Alright. Everybody gear up," John said in a low voice. "Sergeant Fritz. "Take ten of the men, circle around back and come in from the south. We'll spread out here until we hear from you."

"Yes, Sir."

"How is it these here former military men call ya, 'Sir' this and, 'Sir' bloody that?"

"Because, just like when they were in the service they had a boss and they said, 'Sir'."

"Yeah, but you got no stripes or medals…"

"Shea. It's my army. My names on their paycheck."

"So, they're just mercenaries, then."

"Governments call all soldiers who don't fight for them, mercenaries. They don't like people doing it for money."

"Well, why not?"

"They like to control the narrative. The idea of patriotic sacrifice. That young men and women should go out and get themselves killed for their country is noble or heroic. Plus, they can pay them shit."

"Does that mean all these here people are just fightin' for ta money?"

"I'm sure some are. But I've talked to many of them. They believe in what we're doing. I've investigated all those who work for the Institute. Especially those who work and carry weapons."

"Well, boyo' some one sure messed up with this here Maples character it looks like."

"Yeah…well…nobody is perfect."

Sheamus slapped his knee hard and laughed. "Oh that there's o' new one, Johnny boy. I heard everyone thinks yer bloody perfect, mate."

"Alright. Alright. Can we get on with this before you bust a gut?"

As the team moved in, the scouts radioed back to John. "Sir. It's all clear but we're going to need a lot of medical units. We got a bunch of dead and injured. Out."

John called in the med-vacs and started to survey the damage. There were dead and dying men, women and children everywhere. John could tell that RPG-ten rockets and some M249s or even XM312s had done a lot of the damage. He started to look for survives among the wreckage.

"Jesus, Josephus and Mary. Ya think these fuckers were sendin' o' message?" Just as he was going to say something else Sheamus' foot tripped over a body. It was a little blonde girl whose bottom half was gone. Her blue eyes seemed to look up directly into Sheamus' eyes. "Mother fuckin' bloody fuckers." Sheamus knelt down and placed the girls arms across her body. Her right hand still held a doll. Sheamus closed the girls eyes and put a charred blanket over her. After standing and looking at John he said, "I'm gonna find these here cocksuckers, John. I swear on me dear mother's soul. I'm gonna find'em and make ta dirty child killin' fuckers die slow."

"I hear you, Shea. But first let's see if anyone is alive and can give us...."

"Sir!!!!" A trooper shouted. "Over here. Over here. We got people, alive."

John and Sheamus ran to the small bunker and pushed aside everyone. Staring up at John was a severely wounded Max. Through broken teeth and what seemed half a face he tried to talk.

"John...(cough)...agh...John. How many my people? How many?"

"Easy, Max. We're got med-vacs here. They will get everyone to the Haven Help* med aide plane."

As Max, grabbed John shirt he kept spiting up blood on John's face as he tried to talk, "How many, John? (cough)...agh. How...agh...how many, please."

John hesitated but felt Max weakly pull on his shirt again. "A lot, my friend. A lot.....You're the first we found alive."

Max seem to slump a little but then his grip on John's shirt became stronger.

"John. You...not kill...agh. You...(cough)..not kill all of them. You understand? "Save them for me. Save them for...." Max passed out and John could barely find a pulse.

"Get this man to the Haven Help med-plane, NOW!!" John yelled.

As a team of men put Max on a stretcher and took him to a chopper, Sergeant Fritz came up to John and said, "Sir. We have more people. The medics have stabilized a lot more and we have about fifteen people coming from the woods. Some look pretty messed up but they're alive."

"Good. I want you.." John tried to say but the numerous helicopters were too loud. So he motioned for everyone to follow him behind a half standing building.

"I want you to make sure the these people get moved out in the proper order. Keep an eye on anyone who might look a little too healthy."

"Yes, Sir. You're worried about infiltrators?"

"You better believe it. If what Max said is true these fucks had someone who looked like Sergeant Maples lead them in here. I sure wouldn't put it pass them to sneak in an impostor and detonate a chopper. Anyone who is not hurt that badly or won't let you see their wounds I want them to stay put. Make damn sure they get patted down completely. Don't let them on or near a chopper. And don't let them leave. I don't care what bullshit they give you. Understand?"

****

*Haven Help was C-8 super Galaxy. A monstrously large cargo plane the, Roman Institute had refitted as a medical rescue, go anywhere, hospital plane. With four operating rooms, two labs, a crew of fifty doctors and nurses and enough space for a hundred patients, this ship rivaled any earth bound hospital.

****

"Yes, Sir."

"One more thing Sergeant Fritz. If any troops come near here claiming to be reinforcements, start shooting. I have commanded all senior personnel that no other troops be sent here. So if any show up, their bogies, not friendly. Don't hesitate."

"Yes, Sir. I'll pass the word and make sure everyone knows," Fritz saluted and headed off.

"Shea, let's get back to my office. I want to talk to Maples." The two jumped into the truck and Sheamus floored the gas pedal. "Hold on ta yer sack boyo.' Tis gonna be o' short ride."

John got on the phone to Cass. "Hello, dear. Where are you now?"

"We're actually landing right as we speak," Cass replied.

"We're bringing in a lot of burn and firearm victims. I'm also sure there are a lot of grenade wounds. I'm sure you're going to have to perform several amputations."

"Don't worry, John. This baby is equipped for everything."

"Cass. Max is coming your way soon. Please do whatever it takes to save him."

"Of course, John. If he can be saved we'll do it."

****

As soon as John and Sheamus arrived at his office, John summoned Major Jensen.

"Let's go check on Maples, Major. She should be awake by now. I have some questions I think she can answer." When the two men arrived at Maples' cell she was sitting on her bunk.

"I see you're finally awake, Maples," John said. Maples sat motionless.

"Don't you want to know about the raid?" That got Maples attention.

"Only if you tell me everyone was killed," Maples replied, sarcastically.

"Don't you want to know if your twin sister was killed or not?" The remark really got Maples upset. She stood and rushed the bars of the cell.

"If you or any of your, red fuck loving pieces of shit, hurt my sister I'll...."

"Yeah. Yeah, Maples. I wasn't a hundred percent sure she was your sister but thanks for proving me right."

Maples then stood erect and glared at John, Sheamus and Jensen. "You people have no idea. This punk," She said, pointing to Jensen, "was undercover for over a year, yet he didn't know about my sister. We are very compartmentalized, Roman. We learned from terrorists of old. Cells. That's the secret. The enemy can only destroy one cell. The whole stays intact."

"Great! So this here, *whole's* mission was ta randomly murder innocent men, women and children?" Sheamus growled menacingly.

"Anyone who supports the peace between Morphs and humans is the enemy. They are traitors to our race. Make no mistake, the *Order* will eliminate all traitors and freaks. No exceptions."

John smiled and as he turned to leave quipped, "Thank you Maples, you've been very helpful."

Sheamus laughed at the same time and said, "Christ ya certainly are o' chatterbox, ya murderin' she-devil."

"Fuck off you Irish scum. I've said nothing of importance."

""You're right, Maples," John said as he gave Sheamus a stern side glance, "Your people should be proud of you. We'll talk again, though." John started to leave when Maples shouted, "NO!! Fuck you I said nothi…" As it dawned on Maples that she had indeed said too much she motioned to John.

"Come here. I've got something to tell you and you only."

Curious but cautious, John neared Maples. "Ok. What is it?"

Maples grabbed the bars and tried to get as near to John as possible. She then stiffened up as if at attention and yelled, "For the cause." Maples took a deep breath, clinched her jaw tight and began to breath into John's face. Fortunately, Sheamus had been closely watching Maples and just before she could exhale into John's face he pulled John away from Maples' cell. As the two stood back they saw Maples clutch at her throat and drop dead.

"Fuck. Back ta fuck up everyone. I know what ta hell that was. Move!! Get out o' here,"

Outside the cell room, Sheamus looked at John and they both knew. "Cyanide," John said to Sheamus. "Yep. I say yer doctor needs o' looking at."

"Major go arrest the doctor who bandaged up Maples. Bring him here."

"Yes, Sir."

"I owe you my life again, Shea," John said as he put his hand on Sheamus' shoulder. "How did you know?"

"Been done many o' time by ta IRA. Me gut told me she was gonna do sometin' stupid."

"Thank you my friend."

"Think nothin' of it boyo.' Besides, ifin' I let somethin' happen to ya, Cass would have me hide." The two laughed and a few minutes later Jensen radioed to John. "Sir, Dr. Lanfrey is missing. One of the attendants said he went to the Haven hospital plane. Over."

"Damn!!!" John and Sheamus immediately bolted for the plane and as they ran toward the runway he radioed Jensen, "Major! Alert Haven Help security. I'm headed there now. Get your men to that plane asap. Over."

On the HHP Cass' team were just finishing sewing up Max, when alarm's started to blare throughout the hospital. "What the hell is that about?" Cass asked one of the security people.

"Stay here, Doctor. Jim," Sergeant Fritz said to, corporal Dinklege, "don't leave these people alone and don't let anyone in until I clear it."

"Got it," Dinklege answered.

The second Fritz stepped out into the hallway he saw Dr Lanfrey. "Doctor, do you know what's happening?"

"Why yes Corporal. You're about to drop your weapons if you wish to live." Right behind Lanfrey appeared five armed men Fritz didn't recognize. He quickly turned and locked the doors to the operating room. Yelling for Dinklege to lock the door on his side. Fritz felt bullets entering his back but because of his vest was able to turn and fire at his attackers. Fritz emptied his entire clip into Dr. Lanfrey before he himself was cut down. Dinklege, startled at first, acted quickly and locked the door. He then pushed anything he could find against the entrance in an attempt to block anyone from getting in. As he was piling up tables he yelled, "Come on folks, help me. If these people get in we're dead."

As Cass and Dinklege were barricading the door they could here more gunfire coming from somewhere in the hospital.

At the HHP main entrance Jensen and his people had arrived. They were met with a hail of machine-gun rounds and a couple of RPG rockets. Fortunately, they were in one of the Roman Institutes latest APCs and it easily protected the occupants. Using the remote AI system, Major Jensen sent up two A38 drones and simultaneously fired two Monolith 658 turret guns. Their high explosive ammo was deadly. With it's AI ability to differentiate friend from foe, these two bad-ass weapons made short work of exposed enemy units. As the drones were processing the enemies movements, John called in to Jensen.

"Give me an up date, Major. I'm two clicks out. Over."

"Yes, Sir. We took out the opposition around the hospital, Sir. But I'm sure some have infiltrated the plane. Over."

"Then why the hell aren't your people in there?" John shouted.

"We're on it now, Sir. Upon our arrival we encountered heavy fire. We had to neutralize that threat before securing a perimeter. The objective is surrounded and secured from here. I was just going to contact you, Sir. We need orders. Do you wish to attempt to open a dialogue with the terrorists or do you want us to engage with extreme prejudice, Sir. Over." John tried to think while Sheamus' pedal-to-the-medal driving was making their jeep swerve erratically. With the silence, Jensen radioed again. "Sir, Our drones have detected a squad of at least ten hostiles and an APC setting up to launch what the drone has classified as a Grand Mark 2. If that's true, it could take out the whole hospital, Sir. Over." John snapped out of his worried stupor over Cass.

"Ok. First arm and send those drones right into that APC. Then you and your people go and clear the hospital. I'll take out the APC. Over."

Jensen and his team immediately went into assault position. They first took out the three men guarding the ramp into the hospital. They then proceed leapfrog until they secured the entrance. Within minutes Major Jensen and his people had captured or killed all the terrorists. The only room left was the second operating theater which Cass, Max and the brave corporal Dinklege were hold up. Hearing all the gunfire and explosions, Dinklege was just getting ready to radio for help when an ear splitting blast from just outside the door shook the whole room and caused the double doors to come off their hinges.

Though the doors held, there was enough daylight between the wall and the doors for an enemy to shoot through. Seeing this, corporal Dinklege threw over an operating table ten feet from the door and yelled to everyone, "Get back!! Get!! Take cover behind something. These are most likely suicide bombers. I'll hold them off. I think the good guys are coming. Just get behind something and stay quiet." As the doctors and nurses found shelter, Cass loudly whispered, "Psst. Psst. Corporal. Please get away from the door you're too close."

Dinklege turned toward Cass as he put his fingers to his lips and went, "SHHHH." As he turned back to the entrance, Dinklege made sure he had a full clip in his weapon, then took off his flack jacket and laid it down beside him. He knew if the bad guys tossed a bomb in here he was going to throw the vest over it and jump on it. At least he hoped he had the courage to do it.

Suddenly, a voice Dinklege recognized said, "Is everyone alright in there? This is major Jensen. We have the hospital cleared of all hostiles. Someone tell me your situation."

"Major. I'm corporal Remi Dinklege. I think Sergeant Fritz is dead, Sir. It's me, Doctor Cassandra and six other personnel in here. We have no casualties, Sir. Just a lot of frightened friendlies."

After Dinklege pulled all the debris from the door, Major Jensen entered, "We all need to evacuate this position, asap. Mr. Roman is trying to stop a rocket attack on this hospital. If he doesn't succeed the whole place will be leveled."

"What about the patients, Major? We can't leave them," Cass said.

"No, Ma'am. The patients are being relayed to safety as we speak. Now, please we must leave. If anything happens to you, Mr. Roman will have my ass."

While the hospital was being emptied of civilians, John and Sheamus along with a special forces unit were at the site of the terrorist's APC. Still recovering from the drone blasts, the crew were almost ready to fire the Grand Mark 2.

"Wish we had Terry and his sniper rifle. May ta poor lad rest in peace," Sheamus said.

"I hear you, Shea. But we got some pretty good long ranger shooters." John gave a wave and two men went prone and within seconds took out three men on top of the APC. As they went down John and the rest of the team rush the vehicle. A demolition expert rolled under the truck and planted a charge. At the same time two men jumped up on the APC disabled the mechanism where the rocket attached to the launcher. Jumping down they set off a small charge and the rocket fell over the side of the truck, harmless.

After securing the area, John got on a loud speaker. "To those in the APC. Your rocket is disabled. There's no escape. Come out with hands up and you will be treated as prisoners of war. If you do not, we will set off the cr6 underneath the APC. Believe me, none of you will survive the blast."

From inside the truck John heard a single gun shot and then, "Alright. Alright. We're coming out. Don't shoot." The hatch opened and a head appeared. "I give up. Don't shoot. I can tell you things. Don't shoot," The nervous man kept saying.

"Don't worry ya damn fool. No ones gonna shoot ya unless ya try somethin' funny," Sheamus said as he kept his gun pointed at the man. When the four men stood before John he asked, "What was the gunshot about? Before the man could answer a trooper stuck his head out from the APC.

"Sir. There's a dead woman in here. She looks just like Sergeant Maples." John turned to the four nervous men.

"Ok. Who did it?" After a moment, with each of the men taking turns staring at each other, the shortest and what looked like the youngest of the group stepped forward. "I did, Sir," Corporal Kenny Jones said. At five-two Jones' uniform was comically oversize and made the boy seemed even smaller than he was. John could tell the kid had never shaved and wondered if he had gone through puberty yet.

"So yer o' double header, hey son?" Sheamus said.

The young man turned his head to Sheamus with a quizzical look. "I'm not sure what you mean, Sir."

"Well, laddie buck, tis mean ya betrayed yer own ta hook up with this here bunch o' traitorous mutts and then, when it all went belly up, ya betrayed yer new found friends by murderin' yer superior officer. So ya just go where ta winds blows hey? No loyalty, no honor."

John motioned for his security team to take the other three prisoners back to base. Then he sat the young man down and asked him some questions. "Do you smoke?" John asked.

"No, Sir. Bad habit."

"Good for you. Sheamus here quite his pipe after he became a father."

"That I did Johnny boy." Then he put his nose within an inch of Jones. "Tis o' nasty habit. Almost as bad as bein' o' double traitor."

"Easy Shea. My friend gets very upset with traitors, especially double traitors. How old are you kid?"

"OHH right ya are there Johnny boy. Why we had us so many double traitors durin' ta troubles we had ta take us severe measures, we did."

"There, there, Shea. I'm sure this young man has seen the error of his ways. Haven't you son?" John asked.

"I don't know about that," Jones eyed both men and stiffened. He then said in a clear sharp voice, "My name is corporal Kenny Jones. My serial number is 54632." John and Sheamus looked at each other and moved about twenty feet away from the young man.

"Can this kid be serious?" John whispered to Sheamus.

"Ya better believe it, John. I've seen it in ta old country. The wee ones can be more hard core than the adults."

"Well if he is such a believer, why did he kill Maples?"

"Why don't we ask ta lad?"

John and Sheamus then sat on each side of Kenny. John asked, "Can you tell me why you joined up with the Maples sisters and were ok with killing Max Devin's family? Why you thought destroying a hospital unit with dozens of patients was a good idea? Finally why did you kill Maples if you agreed with what she was doing? Your actions are hard to put together."

"Corporal Kenny Jones 54632."

"Sheamus stood. "So it's just gonna be name, rank and serial number, heh lad?"

Kenny looked up and glared Sheamus. "Corporal Kenn....aghh" Was all Jones could get out before Sheamus' fist cracked the kids jaw. Kenny lay on the ground holding his bleeding cheek and mumbled through several broken teeth, "You...can't..do that. You said we'd be treat...agh," Kenny spit a mouthful of blood. "treated like prisoners of....aghhhhh" Jones screamed as John stomped on the young mans knee. There was a loud "crack" as Kenny rolled and cried in pain.

"You know what I think, John?" Sheamus said, as he and John circled Jones.

"No. What do you think, Shea?"

"I think...huh..." Sheamus began as he stomped Kenny's other knee. \

"agghhhh….stop...please." Jones begged.

"I think little Kenny here is just some rich spoiled kid who is o' serial killer deep down. It don't matter ta him what anyone be fighting for, just as long as he can kill."

"Is that true, Kenny? Was daddy rich and you went to find a place where you could take out your daddy issues on others by killing and not have to answer for it?"

"No!!...ugh….no...I.."

"You what, Kenny?" John asked. "I'm going to give you one more chance. If we don't get a straight answer, Shea here is going to put a bullet in your head. Kenny. You understand?" Kenny nodded as he held his knees and writhed in pain.

"Why did you join the Maples sisters?"

"They said they needed someone who looked as young as me. They said...ooh…my legs…"

"Keep talking hero," John said.

"They'd pay me much more than the others."

"Ok. So ya did it for money. Ya killed women and children for money. What was ta job they needed ya for?"

"They never told me. You all took us out before Maples ever clued me in on the plans."

John and Sheamus looked at each other very skeptically. "Ok. So who was Maples working for?"

"I don't know. I swear it."

"I don't believe ya. Yer o' bloody liar and traitorous murderer. John, let me put o' round in this creep. Better yet I'll save o' bullet and let me sweet blade cut his stinkin' throat."

"Yeah. Cut his throat," John said.

Sheamus started to move toward Kenny when he yelled, "No!! No, please he begged. Kenny started to act like a two year old crying and begging for his mother. "Please, please, don't. They made me do it. I'm just a mixed up kid. I though war would make me a man but it just made me scared and confused. I have PTSD. Please don't hurt me."

John and Sheamus looked at Kenny and each other. They weren't buying the act for a minute. Before they could decide what they were gong to do Major Jensen rode up with Cass and four special forces personnel. As soon as Kenny saw Cass he directed his pleadings toward her. "Please, Ma'am. Help me. They are going to kill me. Look what they did to me already."

"John!! Did you do this? Where you going to *kill* this poor boy?" John and Sheamus stared at the dirt as Cass came right up to John's face.

"Of course not Cass. Do you think I or Shea would kill prisoners?"

"You lie. You just said you would kill me if I didn't tell you things. I told you I don't know anything," Kenny said as he rolled in the dirt. "Ohhh...ohh it hurts soooo...much...please help me ma'am."

"Yer layin' it on o' little thick there ya murderin' bastard." Cass started to go to help Jones when John grabbed her.

"Hold it, Cass. Not until he is secured." John gave a nod and Jensen handcuffed Jones.

"He's not going anywhere, Sir."

Cass pulled herself from John's grip and angrily whimpered. "We'll talk about this tonight."

Just before Cass reached Kenny a man from John's office, which was serving as, HQ told something to John. "Cass!!!" John yelled as he ran toward her. At the same time Kenny tried to get loose from his captors but wasn't able. John tackled Cass and rolled her away from Kenny. John lay on top of Cass and wouldn't let her move. "Stay put," He whispered. As all this was happening, Sheamus had been running toward Kenny. As soon as he was near enough Sheamus stuffed his hand into Kenny's mouth and pulled a syringe from his pocket and injected Kenny. Jones went to the ground instantly and Sheamus removed his hand. "Put o' hood over him Major. He'll be out for quite o' while that rat fuck will. Get him ta hospital and have then remove that there poison tooth."

John slowly helped Cass up. "He was going to breath cyanide into my mouth wasn't he?" Cass asked.

"Pretty sure that was the plan," John said as he hugged Cass and kissed her on the cheeks.

"But why? I was going to help him?"

"Cass. War isn't just about killing the enemy. It's also about inflicting mental and psychological damage. By killing you they though I would be so upset it would be as good as taking me out."

"Are you saying they don't think I'm worthy enough to be killed just for the sake of killing me? That's pretty insulting. I have become a pawn in their quest to hurt you."

"Now, Cass. You are the most valuable asset the Roman Insti..." Cass slapped John's hand away. "Oh don't patronize me. Besides, how did you know?"

"One of the Maples twins already tried it."

"Tried it!! Tried what on who?" Cass said, as here voice was stating to get louder and she more agitated.

"Ach, love tis were no big..." Sheamus started to say. Cass turned and looked at Sheamus with eyes that could melt steel.

"Shea. I love you dearly but right now I think it better if you don't say anything." As she turned back to John, Cass repeated her question, "Tried what on whom?"

"Well...Maples...had a...a...cyanide tooth, same as Kenny here, and she tried to kill someone with it. But she failed and ended up killing herself. That's why Shea stuffed his hand in Kenny's mouth and stuck him with a sedative. He'll stay knocked out until we can have the tooth removed... ....and....I...we.." John realized Cass hadn't said a word but instead was just staring at him with her arms crossed. Finally John said, "Maples tried to kill me but Sheamus jumped in, with plenty of time to spare and pulled me to safety."

"Well now, I would classify it as, just in ta nick o' time. In fact ifin'..." Sheamus felt the icy stare of Cass again and stopped talking.

"Thanks, Shea," John said sarcastically. "Cass, you know this life of mine comes with dangers. We all live with danger. Every person lives with danger. We just have more chances…"

"John. I get it. We'll talk at home. So what else tipped you off?"

John breathed a little sigh of relief and continued with his story. "Well, my guy over there had just told me the other prisoners were babbling like geese. The Maples twins were not running this outfit, it's him. Kenny Jones. If that's even his name. He's the big cheese."

"I hate ta break up this here love fest but remember we have ta get the Seally grass movin.'"

"You're right again, my friend. Let's get everyone back to base and start putting this puzzle together and see if we can make sense of this madness," John said.

As everyone boarded the APC, John and Sheamus, who were behind Cass, looked at each other and rolled their eyes. Cass, without turning around said, "I felt that, boys. Don't make it worse by rolling those eyes."

****

Later that night when John and Cass were sitting on the perspective sides of their bed, John turned to Cass and asked, "How long am I going to be in the dog house for?" Cass sat silent for what seemed like hours to John. However, he knew better than to ask again. "I'll sit here without a word until hell freezes over," John thought to himself.

"Stubborn as ever, hey my love? You'd sit there forever before you'd say another word. Right John?"

"You read my mind, love."

"It's probably for the best. I've been thinking a great deal, after my melt down today." Cass then turned and held John's hand. Looking into his eyes she said, "John. I fell in love and married the man I wanted to spend my life with. Then I made the same mistake so many women do. I tried to change you. I tried to 'perfect' you. You are who you are because of your imperfections, or at least my idea of those imperfections. If I were to try and 'fix' you, then you'd no longer be the man I love. So, I want you to be you. The adventurer, the savior, the fearless hero, the compassionate man who cares so much for the world and the people he loves. Who the last thing he thinks of is his own happiness and well-being. I know I'm safe with you in my life. I know you love me unconditionally. I know I can trust you with all my heart and deepest secrets. I apologize for my behavior today, it will never happen again." Cass then rolled over and hugged John tightly.

"Don't change anything for me, John. Be your true self. I will always love you for being you." Cass then took John's head in-between her hands and kissed him with all the passion of woman who knows her man is hers. John and Cass then made tender love for the entire morning. Upon awakening John looked at his T50 watch on his bedside table. It was glowing red.

"Sweetheart," John whispered to Cass. "We have to go. There seems to be an emergency."

"Alright. Then let's jump into the showers so we can save water and time." Cass playfully slapped John's bottom and raced for the bathroom. As they were soaping each other up John asked,

"Cass, have you noticed the high rate of twins lately?"

"We most certainly have. I was preparing a report for you. The birth of twins has indeed skyrocketed in the last twenty years. These high rate of births coincide with the Baylor parasite and the, Sweats and Morph virus. The twin birth rate increasing as each infectious malady found its way into the public sector. Another curious aspect of this elevated birth rate is that an extraordinary number of twins born in this time line seem to exhibit anti-social and sociopathic tendencies."

"I guess that's why I keep running into these freaks," John said.

"John!! I'm surprised at you. Using that kind of language. Whatever the reason for the proliferation of twin births, they are still human beings."

"They have killed innocent people, Cass."

"You know perfectly well there are two sides to every argument or reason to fight for a cause." Cass argued.

"Sure. Sure, Cass. History is written by the winners. I get it. But these people are not fighting for a just or noble cause, no matter which way you point the looking glass. They're bad people, Cass. Dare I even say, evil, people. They fight to harm, to create havoc. They thrive in a world of fear. They want a world in chaos. They don't care how many innocent people are hurt."

"Ok. But at least try to capture some of them. They could be the key to a vaccine or any other host of blood and DNA questions we might have."

"I don't kill for the sake of killin…" Cass put her hand over John's mouth. "I know you don't darling. Please, let's not spoil the morning. I'll go to the hospital and you can go to your meeting. We'll see each other later, hey?" John smiled and slowly took Cass' hand from his mouth.

"Sounds like a plan, love."

****

Back at John's office, which had now been reconstructed and designated as, HQ for Rus operations, more and more personnel and equipment was arriving hourly. John, entered the new command center with a new set of fatigues that had insignia on them. As he sat at the round table Major Jensen began filling him in on what was happening.

"I sent the call to all of you this morning because we feel, from the info coming into us, that the people who have stopped the Seally grass are going to make a move on the compounds in the Seally grass sectors. We think these could be direct attacks on the environmental units. As you all know, between the weather, the mosquitoes and the Chuma flies, without these protective buildings no human could survive in these areas, let alone harvest the Seally grass. In order for us to initiate successful operations we have to set up our own facilities here in Rus. There are two, Outland Seally grass operations just within a ten mile radius of our compound. We've set parameters and built several type-D Quonset units, Commander," Major Jensen said.

"What now? Who ta hell is o' Commander now?" Sheamus asked, as he turned to John.

A little shyly, John said, "Me." Sheamus looked at John's new uniform and saw stars and striped insignia he didn't recognize..

"When ta hell did this happen, boyo?' And what's all this here fruit salad on ya?"

"Well, you said it, Shea. When you asked why these troops and personnel were calling me sir all the time. Officially, I am the head of the Roman Institute armed service. But more than a few people have told me I should use the title. It was confusing a lot of the troops who are use to rank and file command. So the board of directors and several other trusted friends convinced me I should start using my title of Commander, especially when in the field. So now troops know where I stand in the pecking order."

"Trusted friends now is it? Well this here trusted friend was not consulted, laddie-buck."

"Because I knew what you would say and what an overblown show you'd make of it."

"Is that so now? Well, let me…" Suddenly Major Jensen began to cough several times.

"Excuse me, Sir. But...a.. we do need to go over these plans…"

"Yes, yes, Major. I apologize." John gave Sheamus a dirty look and then turned his attention back to Jensen. "Please. Continue."

"Thank you, Sir. As I was saying we've built several type-D Quonset units, mainly because we don't know how long operations will take. If we see the need we can begin to build more permanent structures. But for now these large Quonset huts will do just fine. As far as our plans for restarting the flow and production of Seally grass we have several points of engagements meant to bring this crises to a favorable ending.

"Alright. Let's get to it. Our main objective is to find out who is leading this subversive hijacking of the Seally grass. We…." John was interrupted when several T50 alerts rang out. Looking at his wrist John read that Max Devin was missing from the hospital. He called Cass immediately.

"Cass. What happened? Was Max kidnapped? I thought he was in a coma?"

"No. No, John. My staff said he woke up, pulled out his intravenous lines and left. Walk out like he was going for a Sunday stroll. This guy must be superman. I can't see how anyone as injured as he was could walk a step, never mind out of the hospital. The security said there was a truck full of people waiting outside the hospital and they all took off."

"Ok, Cass. Button up. I'm sending additional security over." John looked at Sheamus, "That sounds like Max."

"Bloody hell. Maxy boy must surely have ta Irish in him."

"Sir. We have reports of a large fire engulfing several buildings about three clicks out from here. There also seems to be at least forty individuals surrounding the buildings."

"Alright folks let's mount up and head out. Major, get some eyes in the sky and bring up the new APC medical and the Palmers. I'm sure we'll need both."

"Ya think we'll be needin' both ta med-armored, Johnny boy?"

"Better safe than sorry. Especially if there are burn victims. The Palmers are in case we need to blow shit up more."

As the Roman force arrived at the scene the buildings were fully ablaze. John saw Max and his family watching the buildings burn as he left the APC and walked up to Max.

"Hi, Max. You look like shit." Max turned to John and smiled through his broken face.

"I lot bettor than those fucks in building."

"I need to know who was in there, Max," John said. Motioning for one of his people to give him a brief case. Max then handed it over to John.

"In here is everything. There were six people in there. There are another thirty or so back at my camp. They're all yours."

"Ok. But who were the six?"

"John you have big problem. I got some answers from those six. In briefcase, they named names and gave up everything they knew. Some quickly, some not so quick," Max said as he showed John several human teeth.

"They had documents, text, emails and signed confessions. It all in there. You best act quick. Roman Institute and world could be in big trouble. Seem four of, Seven Nations want Anaptýsso wiped out."

"I'll take a look at this. But why did you burn these six?" John asked, still mystified how Max could even be standing.

"They were part of those who kill my family, John. They murder over half my loved one's. I was supposed to protect them, I fail. I was on fence about you, John. They offer much money to join them but in end I say no. So they kill my family. As warning to others not to side with Roman family. But I get *otmshcheniye* for mine. My *семья* rest now in peace."

"I'm sorry for your loss, Max. I'll send a unit to make sure the Seally gr…."

"No, John. You don't need people here. We will guard Seally grass. No one ever stop production again. You have Max Devin's word." John scanned the embers and final flames as the last of the structures fell. He then shook Max's hand and patted his shoulder.

"You are my *rodnoy bra,* Max. I wish you and your family well."

"Da. Da. Take care John."

As they team were loading up John said to Sheamus, "We've got to get back to the West Coast facility. There seems to be a revolt happening among the Nations."

"Aye, lad. Never trusted them politician goolywobs. Just look at that there Kolla fella. There about as truthful as o' pack o' Black and Tans they be."

"I agree, my friend. Which is why we need to hurry."

Chapter Five

Operation Showdown

Three days later John, Cass and the Lads had returned to the West Coast Haven facility. It was there they planed to initiate Operation Showdown. After careful study of documents and statements taken by, Max Devin in Rus, John had a clearer understanding of just how deeply and how powerful the anti-Anaptýsso faction was. John held a top secret meeting who's objective was to set in motion a plan which would reveal and stop these people who would destroy the peace between humans and Anaptýsso.

At the round table were John, Cass, the Lads and three Nation's Generals, Thomas, Jefferson and Varma, and John's General, Jim Hooks. There were also three, Nation representatives, one from Tsalaki, Senator Diane Jeffs, one from Europa, Senator Winston Livingston and one from Acharya Senator Aadya Yadav.

"Good morning everyone. As you know I am John Roman, head of the Roman Institute. Beside me is Doctor Cassandra Onassis and next to her is Bubba Johnson and last but certainly not least is Sheamus O'Keefe. I just want all of the Generals and Senators to know that these people are the reason we have peace with the

Anaptýsso. They are a big, big reason we won the war. Their expertise is invaluable for this operation. They will play a big part in all aspects of Operation Showdown. I'm going to let you all introduce yourself to the table and then we can proceed with saving the world again, ladies and gentlemen."

After everyone had done the meet and greet, John stood and said, "In front of each of you is a case full of top secret documents. I believe everyone in here is a true hero and patriot but I have to say this for the record. I cannot stress enough, that if anyone repeats or talks about what's in these documents or, Operation Showdown, it would mean their immediate arrest and imprisonment."

John turned to the security people and motioned for them to leave the room. Once the room was cleared of everyone but the those at the table, he tapped his T50 and the metal cases containing the data all unlocked. "Inside your portfolios you will see documents and recorded statements naming people and their intention to overthrow governments by intentionally and carefully placed actions which would enrage citizens to take action against the Anaptýsso. These actions include the murder of innocent civilians, made to look like something the Anaptýsso did. These documents also show there is an underground group of military and political figures who are plotting to destroy the peace we have been so careful to protect and solidify. These people are in high level positions and have a lot of support."

"John," General Hooks asked.

"You know we can't use any of this in a court of law. All of it was illegally obtained."

"I understand, Jim. Max Devin could have simply wiped out these people for what they did to his family but I can't hold it against him for taking revenge. However, Jim, even though we can't use this stuff in court, it stills gives us a way in so we can start making a case against these people."

"Not really," Cass said. "I'm not a lawyer but what I do know is anything you might discover because of this illegal information would be tainted, 'fruit of the poisoned tree' they say."

"Great!! So we gonna let these murderin' bastards walk away or hide their bleedin' arse's behind legal technicalities? Max did what I, Sheamus bloody O'Keefe would have done. He executed those who murdered his family. He's o'..."

"Shea," Cass interrupted by holding Sheamus' arm. "If we begin going down the road of judge, jury and executioner we're no better, in fact we're worst then these traitors. We are not driven by irrational fear or ignorance or hatred of the other. The Roman motto is *Custodes Mundi,* Shea. We're not overlords. We, of all people must play by the rules or all is lost."

"I must also agree with the dear honorable, lady," General Varma said. "Take it from someone who has fought many battles, many battles indeed and had complete charge of all aspects of a campaign, all aspects. The great Buddha tells us, it can be very seductive, very seductive indeed to think one is fighting for good and one's ideals are always correct ones. But someone else might not want what we want. An attitude of self-righteousness can be very dangerous my friends, very dangerous indeed. If we start making special rules for our behavior, if we make exceptions for what we feel is the correct reality, who will keep us from imposing our views over others, just because we are convinced it's the best thing for all?"

"Right you are, brother. The people have spoken. They want peace with the Anaptýsso. These anti-Anaptýsso officials and military, who took oaths to protect and honor the will of the people now want to impose their will because the people's choices don't jive with theirs. We can't break the law, even if we feel we're doing it to protect what people have voted for. Because if we do, then what happens the next time? What happens when the people vote for something we don't believe in? Do we then become the traitors? Bubba asked.

"You're all right. But we can't un-see what we've seen," John said, exasperated.

"I have an idea," Senator Diane Jeffs said. "Let's set up an individual panel and provide them with all the information we have here. We won't tell them what it concerns. Then we go and look for information which uncovers the reasons for the Seally grass seizure. We can look into the attack on Max Devin's family. Why this, Kenny fellow is not who he says he is. How Sergeant Maples turned out to be twin traitors. We need to definitely look into how they could have pulled that off without inside help. These are incidents we would have investigated even without this information. The blind study group can then check off any item or name we bring them, as long as that info was discovered independently, well then, when we have enough, we can initiate Operation Showdown."

"I think that's a great idea. Agni has just come back from Acharya and his mothers funeral. He would be perfect. We'll let him pick his team, they will have to be isolated of course, and once we have enough evidence we'll make our move," John said. As the room began to buzz with excitement about Operation Showdown John turned to Cass and said, "Cass, can you and Bubba meet Agni when his plane lands. I don't want him to accidentally hear anything about the raid on Max Devin's place or the Maples twins."

"Of course, John."

"I'll male sure the little fella has been kept from anyone or anything that would exclude him from the blind study group," Bubba chimed in.

"Great. As soon as we're done here I'm going to see Mr. Kenny Jones. Cass I need you to run a full analysis on his and the Maples' prints, DNA, facial recognition the whole *schlimazel*. We must find out who this guy is. If we backtrack his bio sheet we might be able to catch who helped him and the Maples twins get through our security precautions."

"My team is on it. I should have some answers for you by tonight."

In the next hour everyone was given their assignments, code words, meeting times for the next week. They then headed out to their perspective stations, offices and commands trying to act like nothing was out of the ordinary.

****

At the airport Cass and Bubba watched as Agni descended the stairs from his flight. There were hugs, kisses and condolences from all Agni's friends. After giving Agni a hug and kiss, Cass said, "It's so good to have you back, Agni. So sorry about your mother."

"Oh, this humble servant appreciates you thinking of my dear mother, Cass, but she is with the great Buddha now. Agni and his family are very happy for her, very happy. Death is nothing to be sad about, it is just another step to supreme enlightenment we all must take," Agni said as he put his hands together in a prayer like fashion and bowed to Cass and Bubba.

"Well I hope you don't take that step too soon little fella. Kimiko and I want you to be godfather to our baby," Bubba said proudly.

""Oh that is wonderful dear Bubba. When will the blessed event happen?"

"I'd say in about eight months, give or take a week."

"It would be this most humble servant's greatest honor to be your child's godfather dear Bubba. I only hope Agni will prove worthy of such a responsibility."

"That's wonderful, Bubba. Congratulations to you and Kimiko," Cass said.

"Thank you Cass," Bubba replied. At that very moment a man and a woman who espied Agni ran up to him and welcomed him back.

"Oh hello Agni. We all missed you. Sorry to hear about your mother," Lara Sims said.

"Oh thank you. This humble servant is very pleased to be back in his home from home."

"Have you heard about all the strange happenings lately?" Larry Fontis asked.

"No. like what?"

"Oh my. Confrontations, suspected mur…."

"Excuse me people but Mr. Arya has an important meeting to attend," Bubba said as he blocked the man and woman from Agni's view.

"What meeting my friend? Agni was not told of any meeting. This humble servant would very much like to hear what has been happening since leaving."

"Well then, tell this mountain to move. There's lots to tell you," Sims said, as she tried to push Bubba away with no success.

"Bubba, my dear friend, why are you being so rude? These are also my fri…" Cass grabbed Agni and pulled him away saying, "Agni. If you trust me or John, you must come with me now."

Agni, looking bewildered, saw the urgency in Cass' eyes. "Yes. Yes of course this humble servant trusts you and John with all my heart. Agni is somewhat confused, but will go with you."

As Bubba held off the troublesome duo, Cass led Agni to a limousine and they left quickly.

"You're hiding something, you big fuckin log. When we find out, we're going to tell Agni and the world." Fontis shouted.

"Is that so?"

"Yes, *that's sooo"* Sims grinned sarcastically.

"Well then. By the power invested in me by the Roman Institute and being as you are on Roman Institute sovereign territory, I arrest you for possible terrorist threats." Bubba then put each of the two in a headlock; one in each of his massive arms. He then spoke in to his T50, "Security, this is Bubba Johnson. I have two suspects in custody and would like someone to retrieve them. They will need to be held for questioning. Under provision 683 we will can hold them for four days."

Trying to talk while his head was wrapped in Bubba's arm, Fontis said, "Yaaa...ugh..yaaa..ca...can't..,.ugh...do...th..this."

"Oh but I can, little fella, I can," Bubba smiled, barely breaking a sweat holding the two.

Within minutes, three security officers arrived and took the two away as they both screamed at Bubba. "You'll see. We'll sue your ass," Fontis yelled. "This is sexual harassment motherfucker," Sims added. "You groped me when you held me illegally against my will. You groped me."

"Right. In case you didn't know I only have two hands, one of which was around you and the other around your cohort," Bubba laughed.

Bubba then went to join Cass and Agni. He hoped Agni wasn't too upset about what happened. But he was sure that once Agni knew what was at stake, he would be fine.

****

Just as Cass and Bubba were filling in Agni about the blind study group, John was starting his interrogation of Kenny Jones.

"I hope your cell is comfortable Kenny," John said, sitting across the table from Jones.

"Why would you care, Roman? And why am I handcuffed to this table? Are you that afraid of me?" Kenny asked.

"Sure, Kenny you terrify me," John smiled. "I want you to be comfortable because you'll be there for quite a while. A comfortable prisoner makes for easier interrogation. We cuff you here and administer tranquilizers when you are in your cell because you had the same cyanide tooth as Maples. So, we know you're not just doing this for the money or excitement. You're a true believer, Kenny. Because of that, we feel you would sacrifice your life to keep secret what these anti-Anaptýsso thugs are doing."

"Thugs!! These red monsters killed millions of humans and they will kill again. It's you bleeding hearts, you shamefully ignorant appeasers, you cowards, who are the thugs," Kenny yelled as he pulled on his table restraints.

"Kenny have…" John stopped talking when there was a knock on the interrogation room door. Having left explicit orders never to be interrupted when interviewing a prisoner, John knew it must be important. Opening the door, he was handed a file.

"Sir. We thought this was important enough not to wait," Sergeant Terry Mallory said."

Peeking in the file, John read something which made him smile. "You were absolutely right to bring me this Sergeant...Mallory..correct?"

"Yes, Sir."

"Yes, Mallory. Wasn't your uncle; Terry Mallory?"

"Yes, Sir. I was named after him. He wrote his Ma and me letters about you and the rest of the Lads. I must have read them a million times. I always wanted to thank you for being his friend."

"Oh, Sergeant. I should thank your family for Terry. He saved my life. I think about him often. He was a man of honor and courage. We must get together and talk. We should be able to find a place for you at the Roman Institute, if that is something you would like."

With his cheeks turning a little red Mallory said, "I...I.. would like that very much, Sir."

"Good. Until then, stay ready at the door and turn off any cameras or recording devices for the moment. I'll signal you when I want them back on."

"Yes, Sir."

John then sat down and looked at Kenny. As he slowly opened and began reading the file, Kenny got more nervous by the minute until finally he said, "That ain't that big a file, Roman. I know this is just theatrics. So get on with it. Either way I'm not saying anything."

As he closed the file, John looked up at Kenny. "Why do all you tough guys think you never say anything? You've already been very helpful...ummm," John said, as he paused and reopened the file. After looking down at the document and lip reading what was on the paper, John raised his head and continued, "Mr. Dan Kolla."

Kolla grinned and said, "Big deal. You found out my name. Four gold stars for the mighty Roman Institute." Leaning back in his chair as far as his restraints let him, Kolla mockingly clapped his hands.

John smiled back at the young man and said, "I think it's very appropriate you're clapping Dan.

You see, you've helped us tremendously, *again!*"

"Right. Because you can run a fingerprint?" Kolla smirked.

"Exactly. We ran your prints, DNA, facial recognition, the whole nine yards and curiously they all came back as Corporal Kenny Jones. Everything matches. Yet, you're *not* Kenny Jones; you're Dan Kolla, Ari Kolla's son. The only way to accomplish that is with help. We are already zeroing in on who that help could be. This is a massive incursion into the system. Not only did they turn you into Kenny Jones but they turned Dan Kolla into a dead person. This kind of manipulation requires coordination of several departments over several countries. You had a lot of help, Dan. But what you and your fellow traitors don't seem to realize is that such an operation always leaves a trail. We're following that trail as we speak, Dan. Arrests and warrants are already being processed. It's just a matter of time before we have all the conspirators behind bars."

Kolla let out a huge long laugh. "My God, Roman. You really have no concept of what you're doing and who you're doing it to. What...judge are you going to get the warrants from? Who is going to serve them and arrest the people you declare 'traitors'? We are everywhere. Before the week is over, a war will begin that ends these monsters forever, and then we will seek out those traitors and cowards who wanted to betray the human race to these freaks. The 'Human League' will prevail. The first thing we're going to do after crushing your red friends into oblivion is destroy the Roman Institute. You mother-fuckers have been riding shotgun over the world with your leftist anti-human ideology. No more, Roman. Your days are numbered."

"Thank you for your time Dan. You sure were a tough nut to crack. I'll have the sergeant bring you back to your cell. If you ever do wish to cooperate let us know," John said.

As he was being led away, Dan yelled, "It'll be a cold day in hell before I help you."

****

Back at his own office, John shared what he got from Kolla with Bubba and Cass. "Thanks to Cass' team we have learned the identity of Kenny. He is Ari Kolla's son and he is a true believer," John began.

"You would think Ari Kolla's son would be more mindful of what he says," Bubba laughed.

"Yeah, true, Bubba and if this was not so serious I'd be laughing with you. The good news is Dan opened his pie-hole endlessly. We now know what the group is called. They go by the name of 'Human League.' If Kolla was involved, and we have to think so since his son is in our prison, then we are looking at a lot of sitting senators, judges, law enforcement and even military who are in on this coup d'état," John said.

"This is all news to this humble servant. May Agni ask why he is only hearing this now?"

"Remember, Agni. You're the head of the blind study group. We cannot tell you anything directly. If you're present when we discuss what we know, then your group can check it off from your list. When you have a full card, we'll fill you in on everything," Cass said. John looked at Cass and she continued, "We'll have to notify the head of the United Global Nations (UGN) consortium, Susan Rayne. She has been a fervent supporter of peace and cooperation between the Anaptýsso and humans. Her concept is not just a peace between two separate species but a unifying synergy of beings based on common desires and needs. Susan's vision of a post-war world is one of humans and Anaptýsso living, working and discovering the universe as a single body of sentient beings. She's the reason we're on the moon and Mars for Christ sake. Susan pushed hard for NASA using Anaptýsso in the vanguard when settling the moon and Mars. Without the support of the Anaptýsso, it would be decades before humans could have secured permanent settlements on these worlds. The Anaptýsso should all be hailed as heroes, not monsters,"

"I think that's part of the problem, Cass. A lot of people feel threatened and fearful of just how quickly the Anaptýsso have progressed. Their superior health, strength, longevity and intelligence scares a lot of humans," John said.

"But that's crazy. The Anaptýsso are working closely with us to make strides in human health, longevity, etc. Humans should be thanking the Anaptýsso. Instead they receive prejudice and animosity for their efforts," Cass responded.

"Which is why we must surround Susan with extra security. I want our people on it today. Cass, you know her well. Take our people there and convince her of the seriousness of the situation. Don't take no for an answer. The world cannot afford to lose her vision and guidance," John replied.

"Susan Rayne is a very good friend of this humble servant. We have spent many hours discussing the great Buddha. If she needs protection, then Agni will be by her side."

"I think that's a very good idea, Agni. If you and Cass go together, then I'm sure there will be no problem with her accepting our help," John said. "We have got to let her know how serious this is. Look, the 'Human League' can and will accomplish their goals if we do nothing. A growing movement of anti-Anaptýsso protests are erupting across the Nations. The continuing propaganda from so-called news outlets, such as 'True News' and 'News for Humans,' inspire groups to carry racist signs, shout inflammatory and false conspiracy theories, march on public offices and politician's homes in every nation. They're waving signs that read, 'Morphs are murderers' and 'The only good Morph is a dead one' at every protest rally. To counteract these people, pro-Anaptýsso groups have started to have their own rallies, often at the same place and time as the anti-Anaptýsso groups. These pro-Anaptýsso sign read, 'Stop the Anaphobic hate,' 'We are all 'Humýsso' and 'Together we can.' The rhetoric from media and politicians is getting hotter and more dangerous.

I know the media and race baiting political speeches will only inflame the situation. Many media outlets are creating and using the crisis as a profit bonanza. Some politicians are using the anti-Anaptýsso to get elected. Both these groups are tearing the Nation's citizens into warring tribes. It has to stop. So, by using the full weight and power of the Roman Institute, we have pushed for the enactment of a *Fairness in Broadcasting* law. This won't stop all media outlets from airing propaganda, but now they must give equal time to opposing views. The *Accuracy in Political Speech act* will allow media outlets to tag false claims, help curb some of the unfounded rhetoric. We need to act swiftly to end the crisis before people and Anaptýsso get hurt. Even worse, the 'Human League' might actually start a war. Susan is going to address the UGN this week. She must call out these traitors in her speech. By having one of the most powerful and influential people on the planet speak we put a spotlight on these people. We can fight them in the arena of public opinion while we pursue a judicial course of action."

"What are your plans for Dan Kolla, John?" Bubba asked.

"We'll let him stew for awhile. Then we'll visit him again and I'm sure he'll have more to spill. A guy like that needs an audience to prove his superiority. He's about as narcissistic as they get."

Everyone left for their assignments, John knew he had to see Archieréas.

****

As John entered Principium he could tell the atmosphere was a little more intense than when he first visited. There seemed to be fewer smiling faces, and many of the citizens were giving him long stares. A welcoming committee met John at the Principium gate and showed him to Archieréas' home.

At the door, John was pleased to see Archieréas wasn't sporting the same gloomy look he had seen in many of the humans and Anaptýsso in the city.

"John, welcome. It is so good to see you again, my friend," Archieréas thought. "Please, sit."

Archieréas then dismissed his translator and called for drinks.

"I'm glad to see you in a good mood and looking so well, Archieréas. But it seems a lot of Principium's inhabitants are not."

"Yes. You are, as always, very observant, John. Don't be so modest. You don't look like you have aged a day since the first time we met. What are you, fortyish in human years?"

"Yeah, about that. But the average age of humans has risen to a hundred and ten, so I'm about right I guess."

Archieréas gave a little chuckle. "Oh, my friend don't... how do you humans say...bullshit a shitter. You look thirty. It's your blood, John. You're part Anaptýsso. Stop denying it. You will live longer. You're more healthy, stronger, smarter than humans. John you're a hybrid. You're the future." John was taken aback by what Archieréas had said.

"Hey, I'm a freak. I get that, but what do you mean, 'the future'?"

Archieréas took a sip out of his drink and sat in an almost meditative state for a few moments.

"John, the human or Anaptýsso race cannot survive forever on this one planet. It will not matter how much we conserve, how much we repair the earth. Eventually, if we rely only on this one globe, *we*, will cease to exist. We must colonize other worlds, John. For that we need a new being, part human, part Anaptýsso. You're the first, John. Unlike humans, you could survive the rigors of space." John was stunned by what Archieréas was saying.

"But what about your fight for Anaptýsso rights? The idea that humans and Anaptýsso should be recognized for their culture, their right to be. What are you saying now? You want to out-breed the Anaptýsso?"

"No. of course not, John. Here, on earth, there will always be humans and Anaptýsso. But when we really get a foothold in space, when we start colonizing worlds; *that* species will be part human and part Anaptýsso. John, remember we were once human."

"Yes, you were, but you evolved."

"We did. Nature knew the human race was on the verge of destruction. If it weren't for the foresight of your family, humans would have gone extinct a long time ago. John, we believe that nature, or call it whatever you like, has a plan for our species. Of course when I say plan, I don't mean a plan like a human architect, no, nature's, 'shaping' of the earth is beyond any of our imaginings. I think...when nature created the Morph virus it was preparing a new species, one that could live in space and other planets. Sort of like a mother telling her children to get out of the house. The problem is she went too far.

The Anaptýsso would be living in caves if we had won the war. We would have been highly advanced predators. We would have never been able to progress beyond that. Eventually, maybe tens of thousands of years from now we would vanish. Humans are smart, but too frail for space. The Anaptýsso turned out to be too fragile, also. It's you, John. You will be the father of a new species that will colonize out solar system and beyond."

"But I'm sterile."

"John. Your people have made it so we no longer need human women to spawn. Don't you think they can do that for you?"

"Sure...I..guess..so. But why not just let the Anaptýsso and humans colonize new worlds? Aren't we supposed to be working together? Isn't that why we're on the moon and Mars?"

"John. I'm going to tell you something that few people know. You were going to be told, but those of us who know you the best decided it could wait."

John stood and became angry. "What the fuck does that mean? Who was keeping what from me? I am the Roman Institute. If vital information is being kept from me, I would consider it treason."

"John. Please. I implore you, sit and listen with an open mind."

Archieréas' calmness and long friendship with John to eased the tension. John sat and said, "I'll keep an open mind, Archieréas, but before I leave, I better know everything. How the hell am I supposed to keep the peace if important information is being held from me? Why? For my own good?"

"In a way, yes, John. Cass, Bubba and Agni thought this could wait. You are under tremendous pressure. Cass said your vitals were through the roof. It's not like we weren't going to say anything; we just thought we needed to wait for the right time."

"So, Cass and the Lads all think I can't handle things any more, hey?"

"No, John!!" Archieréas thought loudly. "Your behavior is one of the reasons. You would never, in normal times, be so infantile. Stop acting like a child and listen." As if being admonished by a father, John composed himself and nodded, "Ok. I'm listening."

"Good, my friend. For one, we are not on Mars." John's attention immediately lit up.

"What…"

"No! Listen, John. We do not have a permanent settlement on Mars and our moon bases are tentative."

"But, why, how?"

"The reason we need the hybrid you can supply to the world, John, is that neither humans nor Anaptýsso are suited for long-term space travel. Both need a stable environment. That's not going to happen for decades. We first have to establish basses on the moon, Mars and then we can move toward planets such as IO. We thought the Anaptýsso could lead the way, set up solid stable living environments and then humans could come in and together it would all work, but a problem occurred which put all those hopes and dreams in jeopardy. You know, for all their toughness, the Anaptýsso cannot survive in the Seally grass areas. Just an hour of exposure and they go crazy."

John nodded his head, "It was the first time we realized the Anaptýsso had a weakness. There was even talk of moving to those areas if we lost the war."

"Correct. Well it seems the same is true for outer-space and the moon and Mars. The first landings on the moon went extremely well. So much so, within four months we sent a ship toward Mars. Unlike the trip to the moon, the Mars travel time was nine months. About two months into the Mars expedition, Anaptýsso living on the moon started to get sick. Eventually they all went mad, just like on earth with the Seally grass areas. Then, six months into the Mars mission, all the Anaptýsso on that ship went crazy and killed each other."

"What the hell caused it?"

"The background noise of the birth of the universe."

"What?"

"John. Whenever you turn on a radio, in between stations you hear static. That static is the noise from the Big Bang. On earth, the Anaptýsso are protected by its magnetic fields. Somehow the fields weaken the damage to the Anaptýsso system. But in space, there is no protection. So the static eats away at the brain center of the Anaptýsso."

"So why lie? Why not tell people about this."

"John. Look at the difficulty of keeping the peace now. What do you think would happen if we tell the world that we are stuck here, forever? What do you think these people and even many Anaptýsso would do if they are told this is it? The fight for every last resource would begin. If humans and Anaptýsso thought this was the only place both could ever live, how long do you think peace would last?"

John sat and thought for a long moment. "Ok, yeah. I see. But I still don't like being left out on this. It's pretty goddamn important."

"John, your family's motto is, *Custodes Mundi*. Guardians of the world, not guardian. You are just a part of what your family started nearly three hundred years ago. The Roman Institute has made discoveries that shook the world. It has been at the forefront of saving the world from itself. This is your time, but this time will end and the Institute will go on. Your ancestor, Thomas Roman started the Institute. What followed were great men like George Roman, Robert Roman and your father David Roman. Each of these men made the Roman Institute stronger for one reason: to serve humankind. They each had their time. None thought they were invaluable. They did the best they could and passed that ideology on to their children. You are part of the great chain. This is your time, John, and when your time is done, your children will explore the heavens and the Roman Institute will continue.

No one does it alone, John. Accept help. Know when those close to you are doing what they do with your best interest at heart. We weren't going to leave you out. We just wanted to wait for the right time. Which is why I'm telling you now. We must begin to develop a hybrid human Anaptýsso race which can spread throughout the galaxy. For that, we need you healthy and whole."

"Well. That little talk sure grounded my huge ego," John laughed. "I know where I stand in the Roman lineage. I understand I'm just part of something much bigger than me, I do, Archieréas. But I'm not going to be some kind of lab stud. I'll work with Cass and you getting this going but I'm not quitting my life. Get what you need from me and then, if anything happens, you all can continue your work. How long are you going to keep this from the public? I tell you, if they find out on their own there will be hell to pay."

"We know, John. We just need to show them the importance of what we're doing."

"You think everyone's going to be happy to have another species hanging around?"

"But they already do, John. You *are* that new species. This is why it is so imperative we keep the peace. If there is war, it will not matter who wins. Because in the end, without each other, any single species will eventually perish."

"Alright, Archieréas, but please, no more secrets."

"I promise, John."

"Great. When I get home, I'll have a little conversation with Cass."

"John. Have that conversation as an adult."

"I'll try, daddy. First I'm going to visit Dan Kolla and see what information I get from him. He doesn't keep secrets like you guys. He's too eager to talk."

"Go in peace, John."

"Go in peace, Archieréas."

****

At the West Coast facility, John had Dan Kolla brought to the interrogation room. As Kolla was locked into his seat he laughed, "What's the matter Roman, scared of little old me?" John gave a chuckle, "You continue to astonish me with your stupidity, Dan. You're locked down for your protection."

"Yeah!! right," Kolla smirked. John jumped across the table and grabbed Kolla around the throat. As he was squeezing Kolla's neck, the young man was getting blue in the face. Just before Dan passed out John released his grip.

"Yeah!! fuckhead, that's right. You see I'm more than certain if I unlocked those cuffs you'd make a play for me. The thing is, I'm certain I'd kill you. So since we need your cooperation, the cuffs stay on."

Trying to catch his breath Dan coughed out, "I….no..not ugh ugh cooperating … with you fucks."

"Sure you're not. Don't know what made me think that." John then opened a file and read, "Says here, you think your dad was a hero. Is that right?"

"You better believe it, Roman. If he hadn't been betrayed, you'd be dead now. Those red fuck friends of yours killed my mother, and you killed my father. When I get out of here, I'll kill everyone you love and save you for last."

"Is that so? Well, let me tell you little man, your dad was a piece of shit, a traitor, a coward a…."

"Shut your lying mouth, Roman!!! Take these cuffs off and I'll kill you myself," Kolla yelled as he strained at his shackles.

"Yell all you want. It's the truth. He was such a coward he wanted to be a Morph. He wanted no part of you. In fact I clearly remember him telling me how disappointed he was in you. Called you a mama's boy. That's why he murdered your mother, his wife."

"SHUT UPPPP!! Shut your lying mouth," Dan screamed so loud it brought the guards.

"Sir, is everything alright?"

"Yes, Sergeant Mallory. Our friend here was just having a moment."

Mallory looked at John and saw him wink. "Gotcha, Sir. I'll leave you two alone then."

"No!! Take me back to my cell," Dan cried out. But it was too late as Mallory shut the door.

John watched Kolla as he put his head down on the table.

"AHH. Dan. Are you crying? Are those tears falling from the big brave, Dan Kolla? Son of the coward Ari Kolla?"

"St...uhh..stop..(sob)...my dad wasn't..uhh..a..(sob) uhh...coward. He...he didn't...ki...kill my mother," Dan bawled.

"Dan. If he didn't you wouldn't be crying like a little bitch now would you?"

"Here," John said as he tossed the file toward Dan. "Read it yourself."

Kolla looked at the file in front of him and then at John.

"I'll leave you for a moment and let you read the truth. It's all there. The forensics report on your mother, why Ari wanted to pod, the divorce you mother wanted. The threats your father made, hell there's even CCTV of him loading the body in his car." John left the room and Dan slowly opened the file.

Outside the room John talked to Sergeant Terry Mallory, "Well, Sergeant. Are you ready to make a decision?"

"Yes, Sir. It would be an honor to serve the Roman Institute."

"Ok, then. Let's get you signed up. Prepare a resignation from the Tsalaki military and we'll have you sign our contract. I can tell you right now you'll start as a sergeant and your rank will be determined by your performance. Just like everyone else. But I'm sure you'll do fine. In fact, I would like for you to take care of all the paper work by the end of the day." Mallory was a little startled. "Sir?"

"I want you with me and the Lads on this mission. I know you'll be a great asset. So get going and I'll see you tomorrow at my office. Nine a.m. sharp."

"Yes, Sir." Both men heard Dan starting to cry again. "I'd better get back in there, our boy seems ready to crack."

"Sir. If you don't mind my asking, was all that true? Did Kolla murder his wife?"

John gave Terry a smile. "Hey. It's better than waterboarding or pulling fingernails out. The truth is what we make it, Terry. Some lies save lives."

"Yes, Sir."

John reentered the room and saw Dan with his head in his arms still crying. He had thrown the file across against the wall.

"What's the matter? Didn't like the reading material?"

Dan let out one last sob and wiped his nose the best he could. He then looked up at John with a beet red face and pure maniacal anger in his eyes. Speaking slowly in a low growl, Kolla said, "You...John...fucking...Roman. You're going to...fucking pay. You have no idea. Heeaa hee. After tomorrow, you'll be the one on the floor sobbing. "Dan started to laugh hysterically. "Let's see how brave you are when you lose the one you love. I'm gonna be in my cell laughing my ass off, motherfucker."

"Why tomorrow, Dan?"

"Wouldn't you like to know?" Kolla said, as he tried to spit in John's face.

John sidestepped the anticipated wade and moved behind Dan. Putting his hands on Kolla's shoulder, John bent down and whispered in Dan's ear. "Hey, dumb fuck. You just gave me everything I needed. So your father was a traitor and a coward and you're an idiot, cry baby. Enjoy the rest of your life behind bars." John slapped Dan in the head and said, "Anytime you want talk let me know."

As John made his way out of the interrogation room Dan could be heard shouting, "You're dead!! Roman, DEAD!!"

****

The next day, everyone was at John's office on the top floor of the Roman Institute world headquarters building. The huge structure was possible because of mega steel and other materials the Institute had invented. The institute's engineers and designers were second to none. With their vision and genius this monolith to the sky was hailed as a 'wonder of the modern world.' It's base covered ten square blocks of New Los Angeles. Rising to the heavens, for nearly half a mile this 2,400 foot building, the Roman Institute's world headquarters (RIWH) was a marvel of human ingenuity. This skyscraper didn't scrape the heavens; it pierced them.

On the ground floor were world class shopping and eateries. There was a skating rink, a museum of natural history and a library which housed more data and books than any other in the world. A botanical garden that rivaled Eden, rose up through the center and disappeared in a lush green colorful haze of abundance as it wound it's way to the top of the two hundred and thirtieth floor.

Six sets of elevators carried passengers to their apartments, offices and businesses. To reach the top floor, one would have to take three elevators. John, of course, would simply land his helicopter on the roof and go down. Those elevators facing the center of the ground floor rose to dizzying height, while people looked out through the glass enclosures as they rode to their destinations. Powered by a Roman fusion reactor the energy was limitless. It needed to be in order to force water, air and other essentials throughout the building. A maze of wiring, ducts and computer systems worked tirelessly around the clock to keep this giant monument to architecture habitable.

"About half of the units were for RIWH personnel and businesses. Labs, both medical and technological, were discovering new things every day. The RIWH employed the best doctors, inventors, scientists and fresh minds the world had to offer. The list of highly qualified people who wanted to join was as long as the building was tall. Seven years after the Morph war, Anaptýsso were working In many capacities at the RIWH. They were especially useful in the medical and eugenic fields.

It was here that the UGN consortium held their annual meeting. The RIWH was indeed a hub of international energy and progress. It was here, of course, that John had his office on the top floor. The office was divided into three sections and took up the entire floor. The layout included a secure area just off the elevator where a receptionist would process visitors. A large room where dozens of assistance workers moved tons of data and information daily and a secure room where millions of files and data storage were kept. There was also a huge conference room which could be divided if necessary. Here was a good-sized studio for video content and a space for small and large conferences set ups. The entire floor was surrounded by thick bullet-proof glass, which meant everyone had a spectacular view of the city. The windows were made so no one on the outside could see in and they could go from clear all the way to black if needed.

The outside of the building was a testimony to art and craftsmanship, starting with The two lions, from old New York's museum of natural history, placed at the main entrance. The entire building was home to carved stone and marble creations. When anyone looked up they would see carvings of marble figures, exquisite beauty that brought many to tears. As this magnificent creation rose, every floor had some kind of carving attached to it. Gargoyles, faeries, mythic gods and heroes came alive as they watched over the people below. Though these statues got smaller as the floors rose, they were no less beautiful. The building itself was covered in what seemed like reflective mirrors but was instead a reconfiguration of the *Samuel Solar Panels,* invented by the Roman family. The energy created by these panels provided the power for the entire city of New Los Angeles. This energy was given to the city for free by the Roman Institute. Anyone living or doing business in the city had free power. This led to New Los Angles becoming one of the busiest hubs in the world. It was also another testament to the Roman Institute's desire to share the wealth and provide as many people's possible with the chance for better lives,

****

John's office was elegant but not ostentatious. A large carved oak desk sat at the back and the walls were lined with books. Original art hung on every wall, including some Van Gogh and a da Vinci.

At the meeting were all the Lads, Cass, and Susan Rayne. John laid out the problems facing the peace and what was being done to keep it. Susan was also informed abut the investigation into powerful people in the Nation's Senate and military.

"Chancellor Rayne...."

"John, if I may be so bold?" Susan Rayne interrupted. At sixty-two, Ms Rayne was the highest ranking person in the UGN consortium. As chair, she commanded a position where she was able to influence many Nation states to accept compromise and to take a more progressive position when it came to human and Anaptýsso rights. She was a strong proponent of the peace and integration of the Anaptýsso community into human society. At six one with a lean athletic body, Susan posed a striking presence. Her long neck and chiseled face, with piercing green eyes was topped off by her iconic white hair. Closely shaved at the neck and sides but with a fifties, Elvis like, shock of hair on the top of her head, Susan Rayne's image could be found on posters, memes and every social media platform. Her clothes, and stature presented an air of elegance and authority. Susan Rayne was one of the most respected world leaders the UGN had ever had a Chancellor. Therefore she was important to John and the Roman Institute.

"Of course Chancellor Rayne," John replied with a token bow.

"We are about to implement what may well be the most important fight to keep the peace between Humans and Anaptýsso. I and I'm sure everyone in this room are gong to be rolling up our sleeves and working day and night. I hope we can dispense with the formalities. So please call me, Susan."

"I'm so happy to hear you say that Susan and of course, please, John," Roman said, as he pointed to himself. "Around the table I'm sure you know most of these people. Casandra Onassis."

"It's fine, Susan and I have been on a first name basis for years," Cass smiled.

"There is Bubba Johnson."

"Bubba is fine ma'am."

"Agni Arya."

"This humble servant is please to meet such a fine friend again," Agni said, putting his two hands together and bowing.

"And last but not least is Sheamus O'Keefe. A true son of Ireland."

Sheamus stood and took off his tam. With an exaggerated flourish he bowed to Susan. "Tis with pure delight that these here eyes fall on such o' woman as ya be, darlin.' Ya may call me anythin' ya dear heart desires, lass but meself, I prefer 'Shea'."

Everyone gave a round of applause, except Bubba. "You just can't help yourself can you."

"Well, Bubba darlin,' what I can't help is ya always bein' o' bleedin stick in ta mud." Sheamus turned to Susan and whispered, "Now I'll have ya know, dear, I cleaned that up o' bit out o' respect for ya. Cause ta mud wasn't where I be wantin' ta be shovin' ta stick, ifin' yer know what I mean."

"Good. Now that the formalities are over we need to talk about your speech," John said.

"I hope you're not suggesting I have you write or edit my speech before the UGN, John," Susan asked.

"Of course not, Susan. We just want you to have the ability to maximize the impact of your speech, now that you can clearly see the full picture with this new information," John said in his best diplomatic voice.

"I appreciate the Institute's generosity and patriotism. But my speech will be little changed by this information. I knew what dangers the other side posed since I was elected Chancellor of the UGN. John, I and many people you would consider being on the 'right side of history,' think the Institute and you, consider yourselves saviors, protectors, even a father figure to the world. We don't need a babysitter, John. The Nations can stand on their own two feet. We of course appreciate the discoveries you share with us, the help in world security and many other fine things the Institute and you have done. But you are *not* the rulers of the world. Your ideas of what a 'right world' should look like is not the Nation's primary concern." John was taken aback by the harsh words from Susan.

"Excuse me, Susan. But maybe you haven't read your history. The Roman Institute has saved Humýsso countless times from itself. I believe the world does need a babysitter. I might also add that we will continue to push the world to be a better place, with or without your consent."

"Be careful, John. That kind of language could be considered treasonous," Rayne warned.

"Yer a beautiful lass, Susan. But don't be threatenin' me lad here."

"John's never done anything but care for people. For you to call him a traitor makes me suspect you," Bubba added.

"Well, you can all be listed as traitors then if you continue taking this self-centered stand. The Nations are independent of the

Roman Institute and will take no orders from them or from you, John."

"Really? Well, Ms Rayne, if you or anyone of the Nations feel that way I invite any of you to try and shut me up. Let's see where that gets you."

"JOHN!" Cass shouted as she rose from her seat. All of you. You can't talk to Susan that way. I'm shocked by your behavior."

"No one threatens my family, Cass. Not even you," John replied. Then, banging his fist down on the table, John said, "This meeting's over." He then turned and walked out, slamming the door behind him. Bubba and Sheamus followed. Back in the room Cass continued. "Susan, I am so sorry. He…"

"Oh, don't apologize for a man, Cass even if he's your husband. John knows what he's doing. But you now can clearly see how dictators start."

"Wait...wait. I understand what John said here was inappropriate, but calling him a dictator or traitor is you being just as bad as him. I thought you were the great unifier? Why the hard-on for my husband?"

"I assure you I have no 'hard-on' for him. He just has to realize he doesn't rule the world. Now, I really must be going. I assume we will still be holding the UGN meeting here."

"Of course, Susan. No matter what you think of John, he's not a petty person."

"Good. Then I will hope to see you soon," Susan said as she made her way out.

"Excuse this humble servant, Susan. But Agni has been your friend for years. May this unworthy one accompany you?"

"I think that would be marvelous, Agni," Susan replied. As the two left, Cass gave Agni a perplexed stare. She then went to find John and she wanted answers.

****

In John's office he, Sheamus and Bubba discussing something when Cass burst in.

"John. What the hell was that all about?"

"Easy, sweetheart, I'll explain," John said with a smile."

"This is nothing to be smiling about and unless you give me a good explanation there will be no sweetheart of anything."

"Mother Machree, John. Ya better start tellin' ta dear lady what's up or you'll never get any pot o' gold from her."

"Please, Cass sit." As Cass sat down Terry Mallory entered through a secret door.

"Everyone. This is Sergeant Terry Mallory," John said. As the Lads looked at each other and then John, Sheamus was first to ask, "Are ya saying this here bloke is related ta our Terry, boyo?"

"That he is, Shea. I want you all to meet Terry's nephew, Terry Mallory. I've asked him to join our 'gang' and he has accepted" all of the Lads came over to shake Terry's and an introduce themselves.

"You uncle was a good man. He saved my life more then once. Good to have you with us," Bubba said.

"Good ta have ya lad. Tell me, do ya have ta same desire for those there gritty things?"

"They're called grits, Shea, and yes. I love my grits, bacon and eggs in the morning," Terry said.

"Well, ya don't seem ta be sportin' that there funny accent o' Terry's. Did ya work on that? How long did it take ta rid yerself of it? Take me fer instance, it's been o' few years but I've lost me Irish tilt long ago." Everyone burst out laughing and Sheamus turned to them and said, "What? When I went back ta the old country hardly o' person could understand me. They all said I sounded like o' born Tsalaki."

"Well, maybe in old Ireland, Shea, but here you sound as Irish as ever," John laughed.

"Hey, while the boys' club yucks it up, I'm still sitting here waiting to hear an explanation, in case you forgot," Cass steamed.

"Oh my dear I am sorry. Terry, can you bring it over?"

Mallory walked to Cass and showed her a video. It was the entire meeting she and Susan had just attended.

"I thought this was supposed to be top secret?" Cass mused aloud.

"It's what I wanted everyone to think, Cass. Only Terry, me and Susan were in on it," John explained. "I needed everyone's reaction to be honest."

"But why? What are you trying to accomplish?" Cass asked.

"Cass, we have to get some answers. Dan Kolla said there was a big event happening soon. I can only assume it's Susan's speech at the annual UGN meeting. I'm releasing this tape to selected sources, so they will assume it was obtained illegally. They will ask a reward for it. It may flush out some people who we can get to turn. We only have four days. If no one takes a bite at that apple, then we go for catching someone at the meeting. Susan and Agni know what's going on. I want the other side to believe Susan and I had a falling out. If they think we have less security they might make a move.

"You're going to use Susan as a TARGET!! Are you insane? How can you put her in that kind of danger?"

"She's already in danger, Cass. Susan knows the score, she's agreed to it," John said.

"I don't care if she's agreed to it!! If anything happens to her, John, I don't know if I could forgive you."

"Cass, I love you with all my heart, but this is who I am. This is what my family does. We are the 'Guardians of the World' and that will never change. I've lost many people I love because I chose this life. I would gladly lay my life down for you, but the world comes first. You knew that when we married and it will never change."

"Alright, you're right. I did know it. Just thought I could turn your head toward me enough so you wouldn't put yourself or others in danger. I know how much it hurt you losing others. Your dad, your mom and Terry," Cass said as she nodded toward Sergeant

Mallory. "But you're correct. It would be wrong and hypocritical of me to ask you to be someone you are not." Cass stood and went over and kissed John. "But remember, I am who I am and *if* the time comes, when who you are conflicts with that too much, I will have to say goodbye."

John kissed Cass back and said in a tender voice, "Let's hope that time never comes, my love."

"Well, if we are all back on the same page, what about Agni? I don't want the little fella walking into something he's not prepared for," Bubba asked.

"Agni knew what was happening. I introduced him to Terry and the plan earlier," John said.

"Wait now," Cass said holding up her hands. "You kept Bubba, Sheamus and the woman you love in the dark in order to get our true reactions but not Agni?

"Sweetheart. Agni is so low key it wouldn't matter if he knew. I wanted him in on it so he and Susan could leave right after the *show* was over. The other piece is this: Agni appears non-threatening. Which is fortunate for us, because nothing could be father from the truth," John responded.

"Ok. So what now, John?"

"We'll offer the tape to the black market and see who buys. If nothing comes of it, I have implemented a plan to cover Susan and catch anyone trying to hurt her. Hopefully, at least one of those ventures will uncover leaders of the 'Human League.'"

****

During the next few days, there was an bid for the "hidden" tape. Bubba got an offer and agreed to show and sell the tape to an anonymous buyer. Bubba was to meet this mysterious buyer at midnight in an abandoned warehouse. Of course, John and Sheamus would be there as backup.

An hour before the meeting, the team went over their plan.

"How much of the video has he seen?" John asked Bubba.

"None. All I did was let people know I had a video which would expose a riff between you and Susan. I got a lot of inquiries but this guy said, 'If it's real I'll buy it at any cost.'"

"How much did you ask for?" John questioned.

"Ten thousand," Bubba replied.

"Bloody hell. The bloke must be serious. How do ya know tis o' man, boyo'?"

"Cause he *called* me, Shea. I know a man's voice when I hear it."

"Yeah, well ya never know these days bucko. Now do ya?"

"Christ, won't you two ever stop?"

"He started it first," Both men said at the same time, pointing to each other.

"Great," John sighed exasperated. "Now, make sure you get the money Bubba. You can let him see a bit of the movie to prove you have it, but then get the money. Shea and I will make sure he doesn't have any buddies with him."

"Why is it so important to get his money?" Bubba asked. "Why don't we just grab him?"

"Because we want to prosecute him, Bubba. If we just grab him, we're committing kidnapping. But-catch him buying a secretly taped video, we get him for receiving illegal property and a host of other charges. When these punks face jail time, they start talking quickly. We want to move up the food chain, Bubba."

"I'd be careful there, Johnny boy. We've seen several o' these fuckers blow themselves up or commit Hari Kari. This lot's pretty radical."

"That's why we're here, my friend. Not only to back Bubba up, but to make sure we take this guy alive. We need answers."

The team moved into place and were ready. At exactly midnight, a figure made its way in to the warehouse. John, on top of the open door riser, whispered over his T50 to Sheamus, hidden behind a second floor bulkhead and Bubba, who was sitting in the warehouse office, "Psst. Hey guys. Our man is here."

Moving to the center of the big room, the shadowy figure called out in a shaky voice, "He...he...hello. I...I'm here. Is...is anyone..he..here?"

Bubba slowly move out of the office and in the shadows called out, "Yeah..,I'm"

Before Bubba could finish the figure let out a sharp scream, "AHHH!"

Bubba moved toward the person and as he came up to him he said, "What the fuck was that."

Still shaken, the man stuttered as he saw the size of Bubba, "Yo...you..scared the..the...shit out of me. I think I peed my pants some." Fred Summers stammered.

"Alright. Calm down little fella. No one's going to hurt you. You have the money?"

"Yeah....do..do you have the vi...video?"

"Of course. Here's a peek," Bubba said as he held out his T50 and played a short clip of the contentious meeting. "Now where's my money?"

"Oh...yes of course." Summers started to hand the money to Bubba, but pulled back and asked, "Is the rest of this as good?"

Acting frustrated, Bubba growled "Man this is just the nice stuff. They go at it real good. Hell, I thought they was gonna start swinging punches. Now give me the fucking money, or I go sell this somewhere else."

"No. No. here, here's your money. Please give it to me."

Bubba touched his T50 to the man's Z50, a commercial version of the military's T50 model and the data was instantly downloaded. As soon as he did this, John and Sheamus came out of hiding and arrested Summers.

Sheamus grabbed the man's Z50 off his wrist.

"We'll be keepin' that safe fer ya bucko."

"Who...what… you can't do this I'm a member of the press...I"

"Wait. What? Member of what press?" John asked.

Sheamus took the man's hand and touched the guy's finger print to his Z50, opening the man's watch. Flipping through the screens Sheamus came upon the man's credentials. "Well. Well. Looky here Johnny boy. This here be Fred Summers. Reporter for guess who?"

"Oh, let me take a wild stab at it, *True News,*" John said.

"Give ta man o' Kewpie doll," Sheamus smiled while pointing to John. "True news it is."

"Yes. Yes. That's right. I work for *True News*. So I'd advise you to take your hands off me before I press charges," Summers said, angrily. "I now know who you are Mr Roman." Turning to the others Summers continued. "You are Bubba Johnson and you...you're Sheamus O'Keefe."

"That I am yer lordship. And I am happy ta be puttin' these here cuffs on yer hands." Sheamus grabbed Fred's arms and snapped a pair of restrains tightly on the trembling man's wrists.

"That hurts. This is outrageous. When my boss hears.."

"Your boss huh," John said. "Is that who gave you ten thousand GMUs?"

Realizing what John was really looking for, Summers didn't want to say anything else.

"I have no idea what you're talking about. I will say nothing else. I want my lawyer."

"Well...sure, Fred. But it will be awhile. You see this warehouse is Institute property. If you know anything about us, and I think you do, it's sovereign territory. Our laws apply."

"What..what are you.. say...," Summers stammered.

"I'm saying, you get what you get when we say so. You're going to be in our iron hotel for quite a while, Fred. There's a lot of paper work; we have to debrief you, I mean you were trespassing on Institute property. My guess is you'll be with us for ohhh I'd say at least a year or so. I'll make sure your cell has a good view of *True News* headquarters. It's across the street from RIWH."

"Noo. You... can't..you" Before Summers could say anymore Sheamus wrapped a gag in his mouth. "Mother o' Christ I couldn't listen ta that yammering' golliwog anymore, John."

"First thing you did all day that's made sense," Bubba quipped.

"Oh is that so yer blubberin,' bleedin,' gollywonk ya. How about me puttin me foot in yer.."

"Boys..boys... Play nice and daddy will get you an ice-cream cone," John said mockingly.

"Fuck ta cone, Johnny boy. I'll take o' bottle o' Bailey's Irish whiskey."

"Sounds good. I'll take his Bailey's..."

"I'd like ta see ya try yer bloody moppet ya,"

John just smiled and rolled his eyes as he threw Summers in the back of the truck. As the two bickering friends started to get in the front of the vehicle John said, "Oh no. You boys," John said pointing to Sheamus and Bubba. "In the back with Summers. I'm not listening to your shit all the way home." On the ride back to RIWH, all John could hear was the guys yelling at each other. So he did what most men do in that situation: he turned up the radio and sang.

Chapter Six

Confrontation

The next day John had Fred Summers brought to the interrogation room. Sergeant Mallory sat him down and asked him, "Do you need a water or a snack, Mr, Summers?"

"What I need is a phone so I can call my lawyer. You look like a fine young man. If you want to continue in this career, you had better let me go. I'm going to sue so many people that John Roman will think...."

"Think what?" John said as he entered the room. Terry was about to leave but John said, "No, Sergeant. Stay here. You got to start learning and now's a good a time as any. Have you been taking the assessment tests?"

"Yes, Sir. Aced them all so far." Terry smiled.

"Good. Good to hear that. Your uncle would be proud. So how about we let you get some real time experience with interrogation?"

"I'd like that very much, Sir."

Fred was looking back and forth between the men not believing what he was hearing.

"Excuse me!!! Training, interrogation!!! Who do you think you are. I'm being held illegally. When my lawyers sue your ass y…" Fred shut up after John whacked him across the mouth with his file.

"Lock him down, Sergeant."

"Yes, Sir." Terry grabbed Summers' arms and one by one cuffed the man's hands to the table.

Fred looked up at John with a fierce grimace and was just about to say something when john slammed his face unto the desk, causing Fred's nose to bleed profusely. John threw Fred a towel and said, "Wipe your nose, Fred. If you bleed on my table I'll break it."

Summers quickly wiped the blood from his face and table. John then told Terry, "Restrain the legs too." Terry cuffed Fred ankles and closed them around the steel chair. Unable to move much Fred started to cry.

"Wh….why…why..are you…(sniff) doing this?" John slowly sat across from Fred and put the file he had hit Summers with on the table and opened it up.

"Well, Fred, how about you're a racist, fear-mongering piece of shit who wants to start a war between the Anaptýsso and the human race and you don't care how many people or Anaptýsso are killed. But you know the worst part, Fred?" Summers just kept his head down. "Fred. Fred." Then John gave Terry, who was standing behind Fred, a nod and the sergeant slapped Fred upside his head.

"Please stop hitting me….I…can't….take being..(sniff) hit."

"Look at me, Fred," John demanded. Summers wiped blood and tears from his eyes and looked up at John. "Good. Keep looking at me, Fred, or the man behind you will slap you again. Fred? Do you understand? Just nod." Summers slowly nodded.

"Now I want you to understand something. You are under arrest. We ca…"

"But you can't arres…" Fred was stopped by Terry who slapped him a little harder on the other side of his head. Fred quickly shut up.

"Good. Just listen, Fred. First, you are under lawful arrest. Second, I'm not hitting you. The man behind you is. He will keep slapping your silly head if you interrupt me, if you do not answer my questions, if you lie to me-you get the picture, right, Fred?"

"Ye...yes."

"Yes, what?"

"Yes, Sir?"

"Good. Now let's get started. I asked you if you knew what the worst part of what you have done was. Do you know?"

"No, Sir."

"The worst part, Fred, is that you're doing all this criminal behavior for money. Not for a cause, or because you want the world to be better; hey, not even for revenge. You're selling out two sentient species for money. Isn't that right, Fred?"

Summers took a minute and then through more tears mumbled, "Ye...yes."

"Good. Good, Terry." John nodded to Terry and he put a shot glass full of whiskey to Fred''s mouth and let him drink it.

"You see, Fred. Honesty gets rewarded. Sergeant, our guest here was a lefty. A card-carrying lefty. Supported the peace, went to rallies, had a blog and a pod cast. How many followers at the height of your career Fred?"

"About a...a..hundred thousand."

"Yeah. Until you got caught fucking a fourteen-year-old girl. Then you lost everything. So after two years you show up on *True News,* and suddenly you're a right wing hawk. How much does a soul cost, Fred?"

"I needed the mone..." Whack, went the sound as Terry slapped Fred."

"I didn't ask why you sold your soul, Fred. I asked how much?"

"Fifty thousand a..(sniff) year."

"Fifty.. Fred that's not a tenth of what you made. So you sold it cheap?"

"Yes...I'm sorry… please, please don't hit me. I'm sorry I'll tell you what you want. Just please don't hurt me."

"Sergeant, un-cuff one hand." As Terry opened one cuff John slid a pen and paper across to Fred.

"Fred. This is a list of questions I want you to answer in writing and," John reached in to his briefcase and pulled out a small box and laid it on the table. "This is a V6. New model. It will record your answers and facial expressions while sending all information to us. Don't mess this up, Fred. I'll give you two hours to complete this answer sheet. Don't skip any questions and please, Fred, don't lie.

The V6 will be monitoring your heart rate and several other physical mannerisms. I really don't want to tell you what happens if you lie."

John and Terry left a shaken Fred to fill out the questions. Outside the room, Terry had his own questions for John.

"Sir. May I speak freely?"

"Of course, Terry," John answered.

"I thought… well I thought the institute didn't torture, Sir."

"Terry. A few slaps and a bloody nose doesn't qualify as torture in my book. Everything in life is driven by a scale. Do I knock someone around for the fun of it? No, of course not. But as I said everything to scale. You were at the Dan Kolla interrogation. All I did there was bend the truth and we got the info we needed. Should I not have lied to Dan? I knew this 'tough' guy would crack with a few slaps. That's about as hard as I go. But I can tell you now, Terry, if it meant the safety of the world was at stake I'd might be tempted to use more drastic methods."

"But I thought torture really didn't produce valid results."

"In the long run it doesn't. The Americans tried it during the war with AL-Qaeda. They got a lot of bad info and a bit of good info. We don't permanently injure or disfigure anyone. We work on the person's mental fitness. People like Fred here crack in minutes. Dan took a few tries. Don't worry, Terry, we're not the monsters. We know the limits," John assured Mallory.

"That's good to know, Sir. My dream was always to be with you and the Institute like my uncle. I'm just glad to hear we're the good guys."

"We are, Terry. Trust me, we are."

Two hours later, John and Terry re-entered the room and found Fred with his head on the desk.

"Here. I answered every question on the paper and I answered it truthfully to the best of my knowledge," Fred said. John picked up the answer sheet and started to read.

"Why the caveat, Fred. What are you not wanting to tell?"

"It's not that. At this point, I'd sell my mother out to get away from you people. You've broke me. You think I don't know what a failure and piece of shit I am. I spent the last two years convincing myself I was a good guy who just had bad breaks. Well, your little show here destroyed that self-delusion. I said, 'to my best knowledge' because if you saw through me, they probably did too. They may have fed me misinformation. I just don't want you coming back to me…"

"Never mind, Fred," John said. "Sergeant, take this man back to his cell and see he gets some food. Have one of the medical staff look at him and check his nose."

John started to leave but turned to Terry and whispered in his ear, "After you're done with Fred come to my office."

"Yes, Sir."

****

Two hours later, John was in his office with Sheamus, Cass and Bubba. "For the past week and just a few hours ago I have been 'interviewing' two people. One was Dan Kolla, Ari Kolla's son. He gave us the intel that Susan is most likely going to be attacked or kidnapped at the UGN meeting tomorrow. With Dan's info in hand, we set up the fake conflict video and captured a Fred Summers. He works for *True News* and his boss is Lenny Murtock. We have suspected Murtock of being the financial support behind the Human League. What we didn't know was how he was getting top secret info out of Tsalaki and the Institute. Terry, can you bring in the V6 and Fred's Z50." Terry entered with both items and placed them on the table. "This V6 proves that the answers Fred wrote down are true, at least in his mind. When I read his answers, I stopped at question four. Look for yourself." John pushed a copy to each person and they read. Cass looked up at John as soon as she was done reading question four.

"John! No. It's a mistake. She can't."

"It's no mistake, Cass. This is Fred's Z50. When Shea took it off him, I had our boys go through it. The code word goes directly to her Z50. She took the calls, we have her voice on file, she's 'Sapphire,' Cass."

"I'm lost, John," Bubba said.

"That's right, Bubba. You and Kimiko were on your honeymoon. I wasn't going to bother you two with this. You would have been briefed but this happened so fast. We gave a code name to everyone involved in the higher echelons of politics, military, hell even some lay people. It didn't matter if they were friend or foe. If they had access to secrets they got a code. Those codes are linked to each person's phone, computer, etc. Whenever a person uses any of their tech it signals a code name. Everyone in this room has a code name."

"Really now?" Sheamus said. "Well if ya be thinkin' Sheamus O'Keefe o' stinkin' traitor then me code name be 'kiss my Irish ass" Lad."

"Don't be a baby, Shea. John just told you *everyone* got one," Bubba said.

"Well I can see why ya wouldn't care ifin your best friend thought ya were o' traitor ya big walkin' sack o'..."

"Shea. I'm sure it was just a formality," Cass chimed in trying to calm things.

"Formality me ass. They were thinkin' we might be traitors," Sheamus huffed.

"Oh, Shea, John wou..."

"He's right, Cass. It was no formality. Everyone was suspect," John explained.

"John, you thought I was..."

"Not for a second my love," John declared. "But you yourself just said, this couldn't be her. Did you ever suspect her?"

"No. No... I never... I...still can't."

"Well that tag just popped up on Fred's Z50. Look at question four. 'List all code names for operatives you know of.' He only wrote one name, 'Zfont' On your sheet, you will see the person who's tech was tagged, 'Zfont' matches the code name, 'Sapphire', the name given to Senator Diane Jeffs."

John then nodded to Terry. "I've asked Diane to join us. Please just follow my lead," John said to the group. As Senator Jeffs was led into the conference room she smiled when she saw Cass and the Lads. "Oh my. I was told this was a security meeting between you and me, John. I didn't expect to see so many old friends."

"Please, Senator, have a seat," John said holding out a chair for Diane.

"Thank you, John, but first I must hug my dear friend, your wife." As Jeffs hugged Cass she could tell something was wrong. "Cass, my dear. Are you all right? Is there something I can help you with?"

Cass pulled back from Diane and said, "Yes, Diane. As a matter of fact there is. Please sit," Cass said, her voice cracking.

After sitting down, Diane looked at everyone in the room. She became visibly nervous. "I have to tell you my friends, the looks you're giving me don't make me feel welcome. Have I done something to offend you?"

John sat on the table next to Diane so she had to strain her neck to look up at him. "Diane, who is Fred Summers?" John asked. Shifting in her seat, Jeffs answered, "I think he is a reporter for T*rue News*. A job he got after his fall from grace."

"And how well do you know him?" John continued.

"Wha...what is this an...interroga..."

"Just answer the question, Diane," Cass interjected.

"I...don't..think I like your attitude, John. And you, Cass. We've been friends for twenty years. Why the third degree?" Cass hung her head and wiped some tears from her face. Diane's cheeks turned red as she pleaded to Cass, "Why the tears? What is it you think I have done?"

Cass gave a last look at Diane and then crossed to the other side of the room.

"Cass. Cass, please," Jeffs cried out as Cass walked away.

"She's upset that her lifelong friend is a traitor to her office and Nation," Bubba said.

"What!! I'll have you know I have been the top Senator for Tsalaki for thirty years. I was there at the beginning, John. When everyone was against you, I was the one who pulled the Nations together so you could win the war. I have fought for justice, peace, equality, and the betterment of all Humýsso for every day of those thirty years. How dare you call me a traitor. I think I'll leave now. I will also inform my lawyers and we will…"

"Why is it all ya's traitors want ta lawyer up when ya get caught stealin' ma's apple pie, now?" Sheamus chimed in.

"Shea," John said sternly. "This is nothing to joke about." Sheamus turned and muttered under his breath, "Who ta hell was jokin'?"

Turning back to Diane, John said, "Diane. It's over. We have all the evidence we need. Dan Kolla, Fred Summers and his Z50 which leads right to you with your voice recordings. The Z50 also had recordings between you and Lenny Murtock. I guess Fred was going to blackmail you." John paused for a moment as he saw Diane starting to shake and look about wildly, like an animal trying to escape a predator. "I asked for you to come here so you could explain yourself, and try and keep you from the hangman."

Jeffs seemed to go into a fetal position, rocking back and forth and mumbling, "I've do..do..done such good, I...I tried not to think...I...helped so many...I tried not to..." She then burst into tears and uncontrollable sobbing. Cass came back from across the room and knelt down beside Diane's chair. Holding her hand she whispered, "It will be alright, Diane. I know you're a good person. We need to know what Murtock has planned. Please, Diane. Come back to us. Help us stop this war."

Diane looked at Cass through copious tears and said, "I did do good. I tried to do good. But every day I kept seeing their faces."

"Whose faces, Diane?" Cass asked.

"Roger and the kids. I keep seeing them butchered by those red monsters. Roger killed trying to save us. Then one by one, my four children were murdered and brutalized by them. The worst was Laura. She was just a baby; only one year old. I saw them grab her and she looked at me. Our eyes met. I could see the fear in those soft blue eyes as she called out 'mama.' But I could do nothing. The red monster simply tore my baby's head off and ate her. And I could do nothing." Diane started to sob again. Cass turned to John and pulled him away.

"I knew she lost her family, but I thought she had come to terms with it," John said.

"We all did. I guess we weren't watching closely enough. Anytime I asked her about it she claimed to have had years of therapy and was at peace with it. Now I realize she was just covering up her anger."

"Cass. What exactly happened? How did she survive?" John asked.

"She and her family were in an evacuation transport, along with dozens of other families when they were attacked. Diane got caught under a flipped truck. Her family wouldn't leave her. They were killed and the Morphs were going to kill her, but our men regrouped, fought the enemy off and saved Diane."

"My God. She was basically forced to watch her entire family die and then was saved. How the hell does anyone live with that?' John said.

Returning to Diane, John said, "Diane. I can't imagine the pain, but that doesn't give you the right to reject all you have stood for. To be part of something that will bring so many others pain and deaths."

"Don't you think I know that? I tried, John. (sob) I tried, Cass. But everyday when I would go to work and meet Anaptýsso, praise them in speeches, and push for the peace, at night I would go home and a *worm* in my head would start to whisper and show me Laura's blue eyes. It would say 'monsters' 'murderers', 'kill them', 'kill them all.' Year after year, night after night. I quit therapy after two years because it was doing nothing to stop the *worm*. I kept getting messages from Murtock. 'I feel your pain' 'we can make this right.' I knew he was using me and after a few years of this nightmare I gave in to the *worm*." Diane looked at Cass. "I'm so sorry, Cass. Ughhh...I'm so sorry. Roger,(sob) Tommy, June,(sob) Sissy and poor...poor(sob) Laura, I'm sorry. (sob)"

Giving Diane a few moments, John then grabbed and shook her shoulders and demanded,

"Sorry isn't enough, Diane. If you mean it. For your children's sake, tell us what Murtock has planned? Is he going to do something during Susan Rayne's speech?"

"No...no. Before. Before the speech. He's going to kill Susan. I'm sorry." Jeffs then collapsed.

"We must get hold of Agni, and send a special forces team there immediately. Terry, take her to a cell. Cass can you go with them, and give her a sedative?" John asked.

"John. You're not going to have her hanged?"

John looked at the broken, sobbing Diane Jeffs. A champion who fought for decades to ensure human rights and the dignity of those less fortunate.

"No, Cass. She needs help. She'll go to a hospital. Maybe one day we can get her back to where she was."

As Terry was taking Diane away, she said, "Please, young man, I just want to get the picture of my family in my purse. I don't want to be in jail without them."

Terry let Jeffs open her purse but she pulled out a pill box and before Terry could do anything she was about to up-end the contents into her mouth. Suddenly a knife flew through the air knocking the box from Diane's hands. Terry tackled Jeffs as she yelled, "NO!!! NO!!! I want to be with my family."

Sheamus retrieved his switchblade from the wall and picked up the box. Examining its contents he determined the pills were cyanide. He then walked over to Sergeant Mallory.

"See here, laddie buck. These are cyanide. Don't ever do anything o' prisoner wants you ta do when ya be transportin' them." Sheamus could see the embarrassment on Mallory's face. "Look here lad. Don't get down on yerself, boyo.' You're learnin' bucko. Hey you're o' Mallory and Terry would be proud of ya. Just always pay attention, don't trust no prisoners, and whenever in doubt listen ta, me," Sheamus smiled.

"John, I've been in contact with Agni," Bubba said. "They're in Susan's suite, getting ready to go to the UGN conference. He said she was just putting the last touches on her speech. We also have a six man team outside her room and Agni is with her in the room. There are two more special teams arriving within ten minutes."

"Good. The hit will most likely come as she makes her way to the conference. Maybe even as she enters. They'd want to turn it into a big horror show. They may even have some Anaptýsso traitors do it. That would really give them a great video to throw to the public and get them riled up enough to instigate more and more violent Anaptýsso and human encounters,"

"John, the damn elevators have been locked out," Bubba yelled.

"Motherfucker. That's got nothing to do with Diane. The 'Human League' must have someone from our vertical transportation team.

"Well hell what we waitin' fer. It only be twenty stories down. Come on lads,"

As Agni was waiting for Susan he listened to John's call and went to tell Susan the situation.

"Please excuse this humble servant, Chancellor Rayne, but we need to stay here for a few minutes. John has it on good authority. The *Human League* will try to hurt or kidnap you as we walk to the UGN meeting. He has sent two more teams and Agni will make sure the people outside are fully aware of what's happening."

"That's no problem, Agni. It will do the UGN good to wait a little bit. My entrance will break their boredom," Susan laughed.

Chancellor Rayne was staying in the royal suite. With several elegant and spacious rooms, this suite was always saved for the top officials and guests. It featured three bedrooms, three baths, including a spa, walk-in closets and a luxurious living room with a view of New Los Angeles that was second to none. There were two exits, each guarded by special forces and the room had been scanned for recording and other foreign devices. Everything seemed well-secured but Agni had a nagging feeling, he couldn't shake, that something was wrong. The only people in Susan's room were Agni and her two aides Marla Gesup and Sandra Hope. They had been with Susan for over twenty years.

As Agni was pacing back and froth in the living room, Susan came in and did a twirl. "What do you think, Agni?" Susan had on a dress which incorporated human and Anaptýsso designer choices. Black in the back with a sweeping front of beige and a satin belt, with a beautiful broach pinning the shoulder straps.

"Very striking, this humble servant must say."

"What's the matter, Agni? Has John's call got you upset?"

"No, Susan. It wasn't his call. Agni has been feeling off all day. Something is different."

"Well I don't see anything diff….wait.."

"What? What is it?" Agni said impatiently.

"The couch," Susan pondered as she walk toward the Bozen Getti couch.

"What is the matter with it?"

"Well. Look, Agni. I know colors. I've been painting all my life. I always wanted to be a painter. I've often thought that when I was fi…."

"Madam!! Please. It is important. What about the couch?' Agni said hurriedly.

"Well I swear the color is off from yesterday."

"What do you mean 'the color's off'?"

"The shade of white is different from yesterday. When we left yesterday, I just happened to look at the color and admired the shade of off-white. I thought, 'Hey that is the exact color I want for my painting of the bedroom…'"

"Yes, yes. So now the color is wrong?"

"I guess I could be mistaken." Staring at the couch intently, Susan replied, "No. No, it's a different shade. I'm sure of it."

"Guards!!! Agni yelled. But no one came. He ran to the front door but it was locked tight. "Guards, Agni yelled again. No matter how hard he tried he could not open the door. Turning to the couch, Agni started toward it and at the same time called John on his T50. "John. We have a problem. Susan you and the others get to the bedroom NOW!!."

"We're on our way. What's up?"

"The guards are not answering and the couch is new."

"What? What the hell does that mean?" John asked.

"The couch is new and the guards are not answering."

"Get Susan and the others out of there, now!" John yelled.

"Agni can't, the doors are locked."

"What?"

"Someone has sealed the doors, John,"

"Agni, get everyone to the farthest room and put mattresses over you."

As he was talking to John, Agni lifted the cushions on the couch and saw a large bomb with a timer counting down to less than a minute on one side of the couch. On the other was a huge amount of nails and shrapnel.

"A few mattresses are not going to do it, John."

"Agni, get under the bed. Get away from it," Bubba yelled.

"Agni. Don't panic. We'll be there in a couple of minutes," John tried to say in a calm voice.

"This humble servent is not panicked, John. Agni know what he must do."

Agni pulled the bomb from the couch and moved it away from the bedroom. He then flipped the couch toward the other side of the room. The timer's countdown was at twenty seconds. Agni ran into Susan's bedroom and told them all to get in the corner. He then threw the mattress over them and started to go back out to the living room.

"Agni!! get under here with us," Susan yelled.

"It won't be enough dear lady. Tell them Agni loves them." Agni then ran out and locked the bedroom doors. He looked at the timer 10….9….8… Looking around, Agni saw a heavy solid oak coffee table. Grabbing it 5...4….3...he ran toward the bomb holding the table pointed toward the device. 2…..1...Agni thought, "This humble servant now joins the great Buddha."

Boooom!!! the blast blew a huge hole in the wall of the suite. Every door was blasted off its hinges. Susan's bedroom was blown apart and the mattresses set on fire. John and the Lads felt the explosion shake the whole building.

"Bloody fuck," Sheamus said.

Sprinklers and fire protocols kicked in and the fire was soon put out. John realized his men had been gassed. He was hoping some were still alive. As John and the Lads entered the suite, there was nothing but scorched walls and a hole in the side of the building. There wasn't a trace of Agni. Hearing something from the bedroom,

John and Sheamus went to see Susan and her aides coming out from behind the mattress.

"Susan. Are you alright? Sit, all of you. We have medical teams coming. Where's Agni?"

"He...said the mattresses weren't enough. He...went back...and..."

"It's ok. Don't talk, rest," John said.

Walking out into the living room he saw Bubba with a piece of Agni's sari in his hands.

"This is all that's left of the little fella, John. He saved my life twice but I couldn't save him."

"He saved many of us, John said, as he took Bubba's arm. "and when there's time, we'll morn him. But for now, Bubba, you need to snap out of it. We got men out there and Susan in there. Secure the area so our forensics can find us some clues as to who did this."

"We bloody well know who ta fuck did it, Johnny boy. Was that there twat, Murtock. What say me and Bubba pay him o' little visit?"

"First thing you said in years I agree with, Shea." Bubba said.

"Alright. Go pick him up. But no funny business. I want him alive, so we can nail all the Human League fuckers. Then we'll watch him hang. Do it for Agni." After the two left, John went to Susan. "We had to evacuate the building but how about tomorrow?" John asked.

"Tomorrow what, John?"

"Tomorrow you give the speech to the UGN. Those *Human League* fuckers want this," John said pointing to the mess. "We can't let them win. We hold the UGN summit tomorrow. I'll have my people working every minute to get it done. Will you do your part?"

Susan straightened up and said, "You're damn right, I will." As John turned to leave Susan stopped him. "John. Before he locked us in the bedroom and did what he did, Agni asked me to tell you and the Lads he loved you. I think he knew he wasn't coming back."

John thought for a moment and said, "Thank you, Susan. I'll tell the others."

****

The next day Susan gave her speech at the 2137th UGN Consortium annual meeting. She dedicated the speech to Agni Arya, and it was a great success. There were, however, several notable senators, and military representatives noticeably absent. They had been arrested and detained by the Institute, and by some of the Nation's law enforcement agency. The most notable of those missing was Lenny Murtock. Though he tried to board his personal jet after the failed assassination of Susan Rayne, Roman Institute security forces stopped him. Since Murtock was stupid enough to land his plane on an Institute airfield it was John's team who arrested him. During interrogation, Murtock was not so reluctant to give up members of the *Human League* if it meant saving himself from the hangman. From there the next few years amounted to copious trials, more arrests and some executions. The peace held and the world got a little safer.

However, the day after the speech, John was with the surviving Lads, asking what they should do for Agni's funeral. "There wasn't much left. But our forensics team did find bits and pieces. They cremated the remains and here is what's left of our Agni." John pushed a beautifully colored vase toward the middle of his desk. "I say we take him back to his home and spread the ashes in the Ganges," Bubba proposed.

"Well, that there be ta second time this week we agree, boyo.'"

"Yeah, let's not make it a habit," Bubba replied.

"Guys.," John held up his hand. "Not now. I also agree. Let's go now. All these fucks are locked away. Things have calmed down. Let's take our friend back to where we met him. Let's take Agni home," John sighed as a tear fell from his eye. As they were leaving, Cass came in crying, put her head on John's chest and wrapped her arms around him. "John, Diane committed suicide. She hung herself. Oh God, John, when will this end. How many good people must die?"

"There's always going to be conflict in this world, Cass. We just have to try and keep the damage to a minimum and endure the losses. If we stop trying or caring, they win. You stay here and bury your friend; the Lads and I are going to Acharya and bury ours."

A day later as they stood at the banks of the Ganges, John, Bubba and Sheamus spread Agni's ashes upon the river.

"I'll never forget ya Agni. Yer offered us yer last money when we met. Ya was the bravest man I knew. I hope the Buddha fella welcomes ya with open arms, I do. If he doesn't I'll be given him o' pop in ta face when I sees him. Rest easy my friend."

"You saved my life more times then I can count, little fella. I love you. I'll always love you man. You may have been small in size but you were the tallest, bravest man I knew. Say hello to Buddha. He'll like you I'm sure," Bubba said as he spread a handful of ash.

"What can I say that these two haven't? You were a good decent man, Agni. Always putting others first. If the world was full of people like you it would be paradise. Say hello to the Buddha because you don't have to return. You're already ascended to nirvana my friend," John said as he finished spreading the last of Agni's ashes on the Ganges. Together the three men watched the sun sink on the horizon as Agni flowed down river.

Chapter Seven

Peaceful Years

By 2155 the Nations, Humans and Anaptýsso, had lived and worked together in peaceful harmony for fifteen years. The moon and Mars missions were developing quickly now that more and more of John's hybrid's were being created and coming in to their own. The first group of one hundred were now at the age where they could begin to colonize the heavens. Just as Archieréas predicted, this new species, called *Starlings,* found themselves more at home in space then on Earth. They had already established basses on the moon and in 2160 they were going to have permanent bases on Mars.

During these fifteen years, Bubba and Kimiko had two boys, John and Agni Johnson. Sheamus had lost and found love several times, but as always, he never lost his best friend, Baileys' whiskey. Sergeant Terry Mallory had been promoted to Major, carrying out many of John Roman's duties. Tragically, Cass died in 2158 at seventy years of age from a new form of cervical cancer which ate through her system rapidly. In the greatest of ironies, her death led to a cure in the following two years. Cass's passing hit John hard. He became a recluse, staying at the cabin he built for himself and Cass. He relegated his responsibility to others as his interest in world affairs waned. Most days, John would sit and rock in a hand-made chair on the porch of his cabin watching the sun set. Occasionally friends would visit to try to get John living again, but all their attempts ended with John wishing them well and going back to his rocker.

On one particular day, Sheamus went to visit Bubba. He knocked on Bubba's door and when Bubba answered he said, "What the hell you want?"

"Is that anyway ta welcome yer old friend now, Bubba darlin'?"

"Right. I think I've seen you, what, maybe five times in the last four years?"

"That's so every time ya do see me lovely arse, ya be glad as me ma ta see yer old friend, Sheamus O'Keefe there, Bubba darlin.'"

"Bubba. Ask Shea in, what are you thinking?" Kimiko said.

"How ya doin' there Kimiko? How's ta boys?"

"They're away at the Roman Institute Academy. They get the best education and military training there. When they graduate they get a commission. Please come in, Shea," Kimiko repeated.

Sheamus looked at Bubba standing in the doorway. As he stepped aside Sheamus entered.

"Ok. What do you want?" Bubba asked indifferently.

"Bubba! That's no way to talk to your old friend," Kimiko chastised.

"Please sit here on the couch. Do you want something to eat or drink, Shea?" "No thank ya darlin.' I be fine. Just came ta speak ta yer dear husband here." Sheamus looked at the pictures of Bubba's boys displayed on the fireplace mantel. "Yer got two fine handsome boys, Kimiko. The must get their looks from ya."

"Like I said. What you want?"

"Look here ya big bloody gollywob, we may have our differences, but John needs our help. He's been stuck up there on that damn mountain o' his and we needs ta get him down."

"What can we do?"

"We go up there and pull him down if we have ta."

"Last time I was there, he just got mad."

"Why?"

"He said that everyone who goes up there wants him to put Cass behind him but all everyone does is talk about her and thus makes him remember. He said no one comes up there just to talk Zen-ball or the weather."

"Alright then. We go up there and talk about somethin' other than Cass, and then we pull him down here. All he done fer us since we known him, we can't just abandon the poor fella."

"All right. Let's go," Bubba relented.

****

As John sat in his rocker watching another sunset, his dog Zuzu lay beside him. John found the lost puppy just after Cass died. They had been inseparable since. Zuzu was very protective of John. She only allowed, Sheamus, Bubba or Terry to get near him. Anyone else was stopped dead in their tracks if they tried to get to John without Zuzu's approval. No matter how hard John tried, anytime he closed his eyes to try to think about the good times he and Cass had, his mind would always go back to her bedside, four years ago.

****

"Doctor Ramses, surely the team can do something to keep her going. The Roman Medical Center is the number one medical facility in the world. Whatever it costs, whoever you need, I'll get them here. We must find a solution to her cancer."

"John. We have tried and will continue to try every possible treatment. It's just that the cancer is spreading so fast. This new strain is some kind of super cancer. We have never come across anything like it," Ramses said.

"But where did it come from? Do you think it's man-made? Could someone have done this to get to me? If she dies because of that I couldn't forgive myself."

"No, John. We are sure this strain comes from a natural source."

"But what?"

"John. In less than a hundred years the world has seen the Sweats, the Baylor parasite, the Morph virus and now a third species has been introduced into the world; the Starlings. When the ice melted and introduced the other viruses they created combinations. Hell, they created you! Now, with the Starlings, we add into the mix another species with it's own diseases and mix those with these others and god knows what comes out the other end. These are new viruses, new diseases. For most of them like the *Fever Shakes,* and the *Meltdowns,* we were able to find a vaccine quickly. But, for example the *Droops:* we are still working on a cure and vaccine. Fortunately, the Droops is not fatal and only affects much older people." Ramses could see John was getting impatient. "But the point is the world is going to continue to develop new strains of viruses and disease. It's been doing it since we walked upright. Now we have people coming and going from space. Who knows what that will bring us?"

"Back to Cass, doctor. Why can't you do something. Slow it down, slow her metabolism down. DO SOMETHING!!! or you'll be sweeping the fucking floors."

John entered Cass's room and went to her bedside. Sitting there he took her hand in his and kissed it gently. Cass's eyes fluttered and she woke up.

"Hello darling," She said in a raspy voice.

"Hello my sweet. How are you this morning?"

"You want the truth, dear? Not very well. I'm dying, my love."

"No!! no!! I'll find a way. I'll make th…"

"Shhh, John. I'm dying. You have got to move on. Don't stop living, John. Don't let this disease take both of us. Promise."

"No. No please don't go. Please Cass. I…I.. can't do this without you."

Cass put her other hand on John's head. "John. Do you love me?'

John looked up at Cass. "Of course, I do. How could you ask that?"

"If you love me, bury me. Then go find someone to share this beautiful life with."

Wiping the tears from his eyes John said, "I did find a lost puppy yesterday. I call her Zuzu. I'll bring her in so you can see her."

"That's good, John but I was thinking of something on two legs."

"There will never be anyone but you, Cass."

"Not if you let this cancer kill you too. Don't crawl in the grave with me, John. Not if you love me."

"I'll try, Cass. I'll try." Just then a team of medical staff entered. "Mr. Roman. We need to take Mrs Roman down for her procedure."

"I'll wait for you. Cass," John said.

"No, you won't. These take hours and when they bring me back, I'll be out for the day. Go home or go to work, John. I don't want to see your face when I wake up. Come see me tomorrow."

"Alright, my love. I'll bring Zuzu." John then kissed Cass and as she was wheeled out of the room she said, "Live, John. Live, my love."

That night, John got so drunk he slept till noon.

With Zuzu at his side, John entered Cass's room but the bed was empty. He ran back out into the hallway where he was met by the team of doctors who had been treating Cass. "Mr. Roman. We... we've been trying to...ugh...to reach you. Your wife, Cass, passed away about two hours ago. She never regained consciousness after you left yesterday. She's down stairs if you want to see her."

John shoved everyone out of his way and ran down to the morgue. There he saw Cass on the table looking beautiful as ever. He went up to her and kissed her goodbye. "I'll try my love. I'll try."

John had Cass's ashes spread on the mountaintop where their cabin sat. He covered the mantel with her pictures and every evening he would kiss her goodnight. So far he had not been able to keep his promise to her. But four years after her death he knew what he had to do. John decided to go on a *walkabout*.

****

John had packed his things and noticed, everything he wanted to take with him, fit into a small backpack. "So much for over seventy years of memories," he thought. Sitting in his chair with Zuzu lying next to him, the two were watching their last sunset from his cabin, when Sheamus and Bubba came walking up the path to his see him.

"Hello, Johnny boy. We brought ya some Baileys and some friendship, boyo.'" Bubba and Shea sat on each side of John. Bubba started to pet Zuzu when Sheamus said, "So who ya got in the championship game?"

"I thought that was last month?" John said.

"Oh that there was the Zen-ball. That's over and done with. Hardly anyone follows that anymore; tis Gamma-ball now. Tis all the rage, more scorein,' more fights, and more blood. The guys love it. The ladies love it too. Seein' all them there rugged athletes, runnin' up and down the field with nothin' on but that there loin cloth thin' they wears."

"Never watched it. So to what do I owe the visit, guys?"

"We just wanted to say hello, John," Bubba said as he petted Zuzu.

"I'm glad you came by, my friends. Save me the trouble of going into town. I'm leaving. Shea, the cabin is yours." John reached into his backpack and pulled out an envelope. He tossed it to Bubba. This is for you, the boys and Kimiko. Just a little something to make life easier, my friend."

"So what ya mean yer leavin,' like on o' vacation or somethin,' laddybuck?"

"Wouldn't call it that. The indigenous people of old Australia have a name for it. Called a walkabout."

"Walkabout what, John. You mean you're just going to walk? But where?"

"That's the point, Bubba. There is no where. You just walk."

"Now what ta hell kind o' thin' is that. Ya just can't go walkin' around ta place. People be thinkin' yer gone daft they will."

"I don't give a damn what people think, Shea. I've given enough to people and this world. It'll turn just fine without me."

"But when will you be back?" Bubba asked.

"No idea, Bubba. That's part of it also. It's a journey of discovery. Like when I was twenty-five. Hell it's how I met you guys."

"Yeah, well ya ain't no twenty-five anymore, bucko. You're pushin' seventy-five there, me dear boy."

"Doctors said I've got the body of a forty year old. It's the blood. Heck, average human life span is a hundred something now, so I'm good for a few years."

"What about Sam?" Bubba asked.

****

Sam Roman was Matthew Roman's grandson, left fatherless when Mark killed Jessie Roman, Sam's father. Born five days before Jessie was murdered, John, Cass and the Lads helped raise him. Sam was provided with the best education and training. For eight years John had taught Sam how to conduct himself as a "Guardian of the world." The Roman legacy, history, the code, the traditions all these things John instilled in Sam. Through Cass's example, Sam learned the values of love, and to feel compassion and empathy for others.

Her death hit him almost as hard as it did John. One year before Cass's illness, she and John adopted Sam on his seventh birthday. It was a legal move which insured no one would be able to refute Sam's right to lead the Institute. John was confident the boy was the future of the Roman dynasty and the Institute would be in good hands. But after Cass died, John withdrew not only from the Institute and his friends, but from Sam as well.

****

"I've left legal instructions for you and him. I want Sam to take over the Institute when he turns thirty. Until then you two, and Terry, who I think you should officially accept as one of the Lads, will keep the Institute on the right path. I have full confidence in all three of you."

"He's gonna take it hard, ya not seein' him before ya leave. John don't ya think the lad needs a goodbye or some kind o' explanation from ya. The kid adores ya."

"I haven't been much of a guardian since...Cass. Well...for awhile now. Sam will need to learn that, when it comes down to it, he must depend on himself. Shea, you explain it to him and Bubba, please give him this," John said, as he handed Bubba a packet with the Roman seal.

"Sure, John. I'll see he gets it and don't worry, we'll make sure nothing happens to him. We'll be there, beside him all the way.

My sons will aid him also. Sam is like one of my own sons, John. I've never seen three boys bond like those guys. There inseparable."

"Aye. Plus after ya… ahh''came up here. Sam been lookin' up ta Terry as sort of o' father figure."

"That's good, Shea. Sam will need every bit of help he can get from trusted people. When he takes over the Institute he'll have the weight of the world on his back," John said.

For a moment all three of the men stared at each other, then Shea said,

"Alright lad, since Sam seems ta be in such good hands," Sheamus smiled as he looked at Bubba. "if yer minds made up I'll go pack me bags and come with…"

John put his hand on Sheamus's shoulder and said softly, "A walkabout is a one man operation my friend." Sheamus looked hurt and John could see it in his face. "Lads. We've had a great time of it. Terry, Raiden, Agni, hell even, new Terry…..Cass. You Bubba," Turning to Sheamus, "and you my friend. I'll always love all of you. Shea, I'll carry you with me in my heart and who knows what tomorrow holds. We may meet again."

Fighting tears, Sheamus asked, "When ya be leavin' then?"

"In the morning, at sunrise. By the way, I've left the cabin to you and Bubba. So try to get along."

Bubba and Sheamus looked at each other. "We'll need bunk beds and the bottom's mine," Bubba said. "And why would I care? Ya think I be wantin' three hundred pounds o' Bubba lard fallen on me during ta night?" Sheamus and Bubba stared at each other, then burst out laughing.

"Well then," Sheamus said with a smile as he shook off the tears, "me and this here big, tall, tan bastard have brought some refreshments. Let's say we drink till the sun comes up and then say our goodbyes?"

"Sounds like a plan, my friend," John said as he grabbed the bottle and up-ended it to his mouth.

The three men drank, laughed and cried into the night. They told and retold stories of their victories and failures. By three in the morning they had all gone to sleep. However, at dawn, John was up and ready to go. He and Zuzu were just starting to walk away when Bubba awoke and through blurry eyes said, "John. Where you going?" Looking west he said, "Over that mountain chain, Bubba. I want to see what's on the other side. Then I'll just keep going I guess." Glancing at over at Sheamus, John could see he was out cold. "Tell him I said goodbye."

"I will, John. Take care," Bubba said as he fell back to sleep."

"You too my friend. You too." Then John started to walk. Zuzu followed.

Chapter Eight

A New Threat

For the next twelve years, Sheamus, Bubba and Major Terry Mallory (now an official member of the Lads) helped keep the Roman Institute's mission alive, while Sam Roman, Jessie Roman's son, came of the age to which John Roman would bequeath his empire to Sam's control. At Sam's thirtieth birthday the Lads, celebrated the "coronation" of a Roman being at the helm of the Institute. John Roman had left the three men in charge until Sam was ready to take the helm. He knew the Lads would make sure the Institute's values and goals were maintained.

After John left Sam Roman was raised by the three Lads along with extensive training and education, he became a fine example of Roman heritage. Standing at six-two, with the deep blue eyes an athletic build with a sharp mind Sam was truly a Roman. The Lads had instilled in him a sense of duty and honor. The regaled him constantly with tales of John's exploits, usually with Sheamus telling Sam how he saved everyone. At Sam's thirtieth birthday Sheamus introduced him to Baileys.

"Congratulations me boy on becoming the leader o' ta free world. Now, let's celebrate ta bleedin' occasion by downing the very life blood o' this here true, son o' Ireland, baileys Irish whiskey," Sheamus said as he up-ended the bottle and handed it to Sam.

"Easy, Shea. We don't want Sam to follow in your drinking footsteps," Terry said.

"And why not now Mr. uppity-up? Is me drinkin' too hard fer ya ta handle now, yer lordship?"

"Not at all, Shea. But you are who you are. Sam here is going to be running the most powerful organization on earth."

"Well then. All ta better he finds o' little relief with ta best medicine o' man could find," Sheamus said as he down another swallow of the whiskey.

"Don't worry, Terry. I can handle it," Sam smiled as he grabbed the bottle from Sheamus and took a long swig.

"Sam. When do you plan on officially taking full control of the Institute?" Bubba asked.

"Tomorrow morning, Bubba. There is much to be done and waiting around isn't going to do anything for anyone."

"Spoken like John Roman himself that was," Sheamus said slurring his words. Sam didn't seem to like the mention of John and he replied, "The last thing I want to do is sound or be like John. I won't abandon my responsibilities or friends. Or the people who he is supposed to love."

"Sam, I know you're mad that John left you, but he was hurting real bad."

"Really? So, all it took for the great John Roman to fall apart was to lose a loved one? Do you all know how many millions of people have lost people yet kept on fighting for what's right? People who didn't quit when things got rough?" Sam said angrily.

"Sam. John had the weight of the world on his shoulders for over forty years. I think the rest of us could cut him some slack for finally bending. There was just nothing left for him to give after Cass," Terry said.

"Maybe but I won't bend and run. Not for any reason," Sam said.

"Ach now. That there is ta talk of someone who hasn't been tested enough, me lad. There are times when anyone will cut and run. I've done it, so has everyone at this here party. Ya will too someday, laddie buck. Trust yer uncle Shea. It happens ta everyone," Sheamus said, just before he collapsed on the lawn and went to sleep.

"He's right, Sam. You're young. We all bend at some point or we break. Don't judge John so harshly. We know his leaving hurt you badly. It hurt us all some. He did what he needed to do, or he would have broken himself beyond repair. He waited until you were old enough to take over. That in itself took a lot of willpower. If it wasn't for you, he would have left years ago," Bubba opined.

"Yeah, we'll see," Sam said as he looked down at the ground. "The most important point is that John's not here and you guys are. I'll need all of you by my side. As you and Shea said, I may not understand why John left but I'm already nervous about being in charge of this *behemoth* the Roman family has created. Being tutored by John and you all, the education, the history. the training is far different than getting behind the wheel. I'm certainly mature enough to know this job comes with a ton of responsibility. I hope all of you will stick with me."

"Of course, we'll stick with you, Sam. Remember we were part of this *behemoth* for years. I owe much to John as all of us do. We believe in him and the mission. You can count on us, Sam," Terry pledged.

"Good. Good. So, let's have another drink," Sam said as he took a shot of whiskey, "and tomorrow we'll start a new chapter in Roman Institute history."

Sam and the Lads sang and danced the night away but not everyone at the party was there for the celebration only. In the crowd was a beautiful young woman, with blonde hair, blue eyes and a drop-dead figure. She just happened to be one year older than Sam and had on each cheek a small red birth mark, undetectable underneath her minimal makeup.

****

Fourteen years prior to Sam's thirtieth birthday a beautiful young woman, with small red marks on her cheeks, celebrated her eighteenth birthday by having intimate relations with several human and non-human species. Tanach Salamar stood a striking six foot tall. Her hair was jet black, and her eyes were royal blue. Tanach's body was wonder to behold. She was a perfect ten, according to her numerous male friends. At her party she was just finishing giving a

Anaptýsso fellatio and swallowing his load of semen when her girlfriends commented, "Woah!!!! How can you do that girl? Look at the size of that dick."

Tanach wiped her mouth and replied, "Ughh...You have no idea how good they're cum tastes. It's better than candy and there is sooo much."

"No way," Jim Sanders said. "I can fill a shot glass."

Tanach laughed as she began to put a condom on another Anaptýsso hard penis. "Yeah sure, you can fill a shot glass, Jimmy and that's pretty good for a human but my guy here can fill a coffee mug."

"You better be careful. That thing gets in your twat and you're dead," Cindy Morgan said.

"You think I don't know that. But fucking is just too boring. I need danger. Anyway, I have more than one-hole Cindy. My red devils only get the brown eye," Tanach said as she guided the Anaptýsso into her anus. Ohhhh yeah that's so...so...ugh...so. Cindy... ugh get Jimmy boy...ugh hard... I want him in...ugh my... ugh...my gush. Ugh...NOW."

As soon as Jim got hard, he entered Tanach's pussy. As she rode both cocks, she thought of only two things, how good the dicks felt in her and how sweet her revenge on the Roman empire, starting with Sam Roman, would be. She knew her mother, Tamar Roman and her father, Mark Roman would be proud of what she was going to do; bring down John Roman's world.

****

A few weeks into Sam's running the Institute the security division was getting some disturbing reports. Major Terry Mallory brought these to Sam's attention. In a meeting which included Sheamus and Bubba the four discussed the incidents.

"What we've got here is a series of events which to say the least seem odd," Terry started, "There have been sightings of Anaptýsso having sex with human men and women. Both the human and Anaptýsso are young and according to witnesses who know them, rebellious. There are also a growing number of anti-Starling groups. These groups want the Nations to stop cloning Starlings and bring back any who are in space or on the moon or Mars, back to earth."

"Are they crazy or fanatics, Terry. Who in their right mind would want to end the Starlings? They are the future of 'Humýsso'," Sam asked.

"I agree, Sam. But these groups don't want to be part of Humýsso. They say the very word is offensive. They want human and Anaptýsso put back in the lexicon. They also want Starlings to be terminated," Terry said.

Standing up and with a very angry voice Sam said, "That's genocide talk and that's treason."

Turning to Bubba and Sheamus, Sam ordered, "Guys go find out who runs these organizations. Identify the leaders and Terry will pick them up. Terry, how many groups have you identified so far and what's their numbers look like?"

"As of now there are two major groups the, 'Never Starling' and the 'Human and Anaptýsso United.' The number one tenet for all these groups is: the elimination of Starlings. Who they consider the greatest danger to both humans and Anaptýsso. They also believe the name, Humýsso to be detrimental to the human and Anaptýsso species. They think the word not only doesn't unite the two species it actually diminishes each of their cultural, philosophical and physical differences.

They want the terms human and Anaptýsso which used to describe them put back into the official lexicon.

"That figures. Most anti-fill-in-the-blank rabble are hypocrites at best. These are the very same fucks who hated each other before the war and the Starlings were created," Bubba smirked.

"Some, Bubba. However, many great social changes have been made by dissident organizations. My problem comes with anyone calling for harm or death to another person. We will not stand for that kind of dissent. It's dangerous to the state and treasonous to the very foundation of what the world is trying to achieve," Sam said distraughtly. "I'm still not exactly sure what everyone's problem with the Starlings is. There has been no new cloning of Starlings for ten years. They are happily reproducing themselves. They have opened the universe to all of us. Something that would have taken centuries to accomplish, the Starlings have done in a decade. We are on the moon permanently, Mars is a decade, at the most, from being a fully settled planet. Hell, I'll bet within two years there will be a Martian birth. The Starlings have sent us invaluable scientific data, minerals from the moon, Mars and asteroid mining. The whole process has been a dream come true for earth's population. The Starlings are the key to all of Humýssoian future."

"Well, yeah. But what happens if the Starlings start thinking Humýssos are just a big waste of space? Excuse the pun," Terry said.

"How so, Terry?" Sam asked.

"How would you feel if your species was doing all the work? Was healthier, stronger, smarter and particularly well adapted to space exploration? But you keep shipping, and sharing, the fruits of your labor to what some may consider an inferior species. Now, consider your species has to depend on the benevolent grace of said superior species. You want to live under that 'state of grace'?" Terry answered. Sam thought some and said,

"I see that as a pretty negative way of looking at the situation. We are all from human origins. The Anaptýsso were human. They and we humans saw the light of cooperation after the war. The Starlings were created from the very DNA of John Roman, himself a product of human and Anaptýsso blood. John was the first Starling. I believe the Starlings are far above the pettiness of humans and even Anaptýsso. They have the universe, why would they abandon or hurt their parents? I have faith in the Starlings. I do know one thing for sure. The best way to get Starlings to hurt Humýssoians is for us to attack them first," Sam ended.

"Hey I'm with you. But there is a lot of talk going on behind the scenes," Terry warned.

"If what you say is true that talk could easily turn to treason. We will not be threatened by those with unfounded fears of Starlings. We and the Starlings will continue to work together in peace and any who try to interfere in that mission will suffer the consequence. The Starlings are our friends, our...children and will continue to be so," Sam finished.

Turning away, Terry whispered to himself, "Tell that to the Neanderthals."

Breaking the silence Sheamus said, "Don't worry yerself now, Sam me lad. Sheamus here will find out what ta hell's goin' on. These bloody womps won't suspect an old Zuzudosh like me ta be o' spy. In fact I'm just ta kind o' fella they'd be expectin' ta believe their shite."

"Sounds good, guys. So, Terry, you work the official side, Bubba, find out what you can on the public side and Shea, you go undercover. We'll all meet here in a week, and see what we can do about this. We need to stop this dangerous nonsense as quickly as possible. While you all are doing your job I'll have my people on this end and start a PR campaign lauding the success of cooperation among humans, Anaptýsso and Starlings. On the other end, we'll put out numerous ads against the anti-Starling factions. So let's get busy guys," Sam ended the meeting and everyone went their separate ways.

****

Not far from RIWH where Sam and the Lads had just planned their moves against the anti-Starling movement, Tanach Roman was seeking to secure alliances with powerful politicians and military people. She, of course, used the two things her parents Mark and Tamar Roman taught her. As her mother Tamar Roman did before her, Tanach used her body and sexuality, gaining favor with many young Anaptýsso and humans. Like her father, Mark Roman, Tanach could sniff out weakness's such as greed, revenge, hate or various other negative Humýsso traits. Like her father, Tanach had that ability and she used it well. The same way Lenny Murtock used revenge to turn Diane Jeffs, Tanach secured three senators wanting revenge. She also had two high-level military people in her pocket, using their fear of what Starlings might to do once they colonize the inner planets.

With the growing list of humans and Anaptýsso joining her fight, Tanach was ready to set the final stage of her plans in motion. The first part of the plan was to seduce Sam Roman.

"I'm going to enjoy fucking and then killing that privileged white boy," Tanach thought. Since Mark and Tamar kept Tanach's birth a secret, no one knew her true identity. She had gone under the name Tanach Salamar all her life. With an air-tight backstory, anyone investigating her past would find an orphaned girl who was raised at the 'Salamar Home for Wayward Children'. Tanach took the name of the home for her surname. Though she was only two when her parents died, Mark and Tamar had left dozens of videos which helped shape their child's personality. With the aid of Unter Salamar, also an alias, and a former ally of Mark Roman, further endowed Tanach with a hatred for all the Roman family. Tanach's determination to destroy the Roman Institute and its family was complete.

****

On a sunny afternoon a week after his meeting with the Lads, Sam happened to bump into Tanach as he maked his way to his top floor office. Tanach had put on a pair of big oval glasses, though she didn't need them, she also put her hair up in a bun, and wore half her usual make-up. She toned down her typical sexy clothing, but kept the tight black office dress. Accenting this new look was a pair of black, very sexy, heeled shoes. It was a move to make Sam think of her as a 'good girl,' yet, her attire still oozed sex. It was a perfect trap and it worked.

"Oh excuse me Miss," Sam said as he helped Tanach pick up the files he had knocked out of her arms. As they both knelt face to face, Tanach moved her glasses back up, looked into Sam's eyes and with a sultry voice said, "No it's alright. I'm sooo dang clumsy."

In that moment Sam was hooked. For him it was love at first sight. He wanted to swim in those blue eyes. As the two stood, Sam stuttered, "Look...le...let me make it up to you. How...about...ugh...dinn?"

"Dinner? I'd love to, Mr. Roman, but aren't you busy?"

"You know who I am?"

"Of course Mr. R..."

"No. No. Please. Sam."

"Alright, Sam. Yes of course I know who you are. I'd be a pretty bad employee If I didn't know what my boss looked like." As the two talked, Sam's aides kept trying to get him to move. "Mr. Roman we really need to go. The council is waiting, Sir."

"See. I knew you were busy," Tanach reached into her purse, pulled out a pen and wrote her number on Sam's hand, "Here. Call me when you have some time, Sam," Tanach smiled, turned and walked away making sure her hips swung just the right amount.

****

At the RIWH security division, Terry was assessing intel which made him nervous.

"Sergeant Vannor, what do you make of this?"

Scanning the documents, Sergeant Allie Vannor saw a pattern which piqued her curiosity.

"Well, Sir, these movements here and here. Who authorized them and why the concentration on the moon and all Starling staging areas?"

"Exactly what I thought, Sergeant. Lets find out who's behind these movements, who's in charger of those troops, and what their mission is. Do it quietly Sergeant. I don't want to raise suspicions."

"Yes, Sir. I'm amazed they thought they could get away with whatever they're trying without someone noticing," Vannor said.

"You're pretty new here, Vannor. When we said this division was top secret we weren't just blowing smoke. We check and recheck data and intel that would normally end at other security sectors. We're the ultimate stop gap for nefarious doings, in our and other Nation's military."

"Isn't that spying, Sir?"

"We prefer to call it 'looking out for our friends.'"

****

As Terry had his people look into the movement of military units, Sam held a political get-together at his estate on the West coast. Many of the key players in office, advisors, powerful corporate executives, and representatives from all eight Nations were in attendance. Sam had also invited Tanach but two hours into the soiree she hadn't shown. Sam was listening to Senator Grimes, from the nation of Europa drone on about something but he didn't hear Grimes and his eyes kept looking at the door. Finally, Senator Lisa Grimes said, "I dare say, Sam, that you haven't heard a word I've spoken, dear boy."

Turning to Grimes, Sam stuttered, "Oh….a...yes...yes...I'm sorry Senator...my mind has been a little preoccupied with …"

Suddenly the room went silent as Tanach entered. Wearing a long, tightly-fit red dress, with a slit that went to her upper thigh. Tanach's entrance stopped the room cold. Her lush black hair, with big curls seemed to bloom from all sides of her head. Here blue eyes pierced the room. Around her neck was a diamond encrusted necklace which fell on a bosom elevated by her dress' push-up bra. Tanach's bare neck, arms and shoulders revealed her lovely golden brown flawless skin. Her body hugging dress showed off her fit physique and her black strapped stiletto-heeled shoes made her more statuesque and enticingly sexy.

Sam turned to see why the room had suddenly ceased talking and when he laid eyes on Tanach he thought, "I'm gong to marry her."

"Well my friend, I see what your mind was occupied with," Grimes said with a smile.

"Oh, yes, Senator Grimes. Please excuse me," Sam said turning and walking toward Tanach. Of course, by this time, several young and old men had surrounded Tanach asking her questions about her, significant other status, but Sam quickly cleared the 'mob' and soon had Tanach to himself.

"I didn't think you were coming, Tanach," Sam asked.

"Mr. Roman I wouldn…"

"No. Please," Sam pleaded as he took Tanach's hand. "Please. Just Sam. I don't want there to be a 'mister' between us."

Tanach smiled as she stared into Sam's eyes. "I would like that a lot. Sam."

The two then went to sit at the main table. There, Sam had Terry's placed moved so Tanach could sit next to him. The meeting was a typical conference, party style get-together, combining bad jokes and serious issues. After breaking into groups, most people moved to different corners of the room while more food and drink was offered and a small orchestra played the classics softly in the background. Many deals and promises were made during this time but the only thing Sam was interested in was Tanach.

"I must be honest with you, Tanach. I have never felt this way about anyone before. I can't explain it. There's just something about you."

"Wow. Sam, you're saying all this, and you haven't even gotten into my panties yet," Tanach said as she stroked Sam's leg.

Sam's face flushed and his penis got hard as a rock. He started to breathe quickly and as Tanach leaned over and stuck her tongue in his ear Sam exploded in his pants, "Oh fuck," Sam cursed.

"Yessss...I dooo...Sam," Tanach cooed. "Why don't we go somewhere private and I'll help you clean up and we can start fresh.

Sam led Tanach into his suite and the second he locked the door she stripped his pants off and licked up his ejaculation. Then she started to get him hard again using her tongue and lips. Shoving Sam's large penis down her throat. Sam nearly went comatose from pleasure. He came again as Tanach swallowed all of it. Them she stood and kissed Sam as she stripped her own clothes off. As Tanach led him by his rising dick to the bed, Sam admired the magnificence of her body.

As she lay Sam down on the bed, Tanach mounted his hard penis and rode Sam for ten minutes. She moaned with pleasure and Sam accompanied her with his own groaning. Together their song of sex could be heard by those near the suite. The older diplomats talked about past encounters and the younger one's bragged about their recent exploits. Many discreetly moved away, giving the couple privacy. About an hour later there was only silence from the lovemaking boudoir. None in attendance had ever seen Sam Roman behave in such a way before. Senator Grimes commented, "I guess we should all start looking for wedding presents, hey, ladies and gentlemen?" Everyone raised a glass in a toast and were waiting for the two to reappear.

However, inside Sam's room it was quite a different story. Sam was the only occupant and as he lay on the master bed, the last drop of his blood was flowing from his throat. Moments earlier as Tanach sat on top of Sam's body she looked into his eyes and cooed, "You have penetrated every hole my body possesses. You have a magnificent prick. I orgasmed three times. It will be such a shame to never use it again.

"No Tanach, you will be able to use it whenever you wish. I want to marry you, Tanach. Please! Do me the honor of being my life partner."

"Right, and what would all your security people say? I'd be put under a microscope and be watched night and day. Besides, Sam. We just met. I could be here to kill you. You just never know about people," Tanach re-straddled Sam's body and as she looked down into his eyes she smiled, saying, "The Roman family thinks they're soo...sooo...very smart. But you *did* let a killer like me into your bed." Sam was confused. He tried to get up, but found he could not move, "Shh. Sam," Tanach purred as she put her finger against Sam's lips. You will never move again, my dear. The narcotic I slipped you is very powerful and before it can wear off, I am going to slit your throat. Unable to move a muscle or utter a sound, Sam felt only rage and shame. He had let his guard down. His anger at John had left him looking for someone to love and found the wrong person. Now, here was a threat to the whole Roman Institute and he was about to be slaughtered. His place in history, his failure was all he could think about. He was helpless and no cavalry was going to save him. No matter how hard he tried, he couldn't move or think of a way out. As he was deep in thought, Tanach slapped him hard across his face.

"Snap out of it Sam. No one's coming. I want you to hear this. Your precious Starlings will eventually destroy humanity and the Anaptýsso. As always, you Romans think only about your great Eden. We're not going to let that happen. The Starlings will be destroyed within two months. Then it will be *MY* father's name, Mark Roman, who will helm the Roman Institute for the next millennia. It will be his vision which will guide the world. Just think Sam, it will be your death which sparks the outrage against the Starlings. I've left just the right amount of evidence to suggest a Starling did this. With our news outlets filling the airwaves with anti-Starling messaging, we will turn public opinion around quickly. We have people in the UGN and the military who will help rid us of this Starling plague." Tanach pulled a Starling ceremonial knife from behind her back and as she moved it to Sam's throat his mind dove deep into himself. He remembered what Agni had taught him and he let his mind think of only one thing. There was no fear, no anger, no regret, no hate for John or this woman killing him. All there was in Sam's heart, as the knife slid across his neck, was love and all that was in his mind was one word: Tanach.

    As Sam lay dead, Tanach, who had been given the code by an inside ally, opened Sam's personal elevator and took it to the ground floor. When the doors opened, both of the elevator's guards were gone, replaced by Tanach's people. Leaving the private elevator, Tanach set the timer on a powerful bomb she had planted. She and the two impostors easily moved to the main entrance and disappeared into the crowd. Seven minutes later, a huge explosion rocked RIWH. It was the first time in the iconic building's history that it had been attacked.

Chapter Nine

New Heroes

At Sam's funeral, the Lads delivered their eulogies with great reverence. "I knew Sam since the day he was born. He grew up a true Roman. He believed in its motto *Custodes Mundi* with all his heart and soul. John believed in him to. He made Sam the sole heir to the Roman Institute's future endeavors. Sam Roman would have been one of the great ones. However, the forces of evil took him from us. But, I, Bubba Jonson, swear this to the thousands of you here: I will not stop until justice is done. Rest in peace Sam."

"My name is Major Terry Mallory. I was Sam's security and I failed him. I failed a great man, a great leader, a great friend. I have offered my resignation. Whether accepted or not, I will fight every day of my life to bring these killers to justice. Rest easy Sam, I'll see you in the next world."

Bubba's twin son's, John and Agni Johnson had grown up to be fine young men. They both stood at six-four with jet black hair, beautiful brown skin and slightly slanted almond eyes. With muscular athletic builds and possessing sharp minds John and Agni Johnson had a great future ahead of them. Despite their father not wanting them to get involved in Institute politics the two young men were determined to join the fight for all beings; whether human, Anaptýsso or Starling. Against their father's will they spoke at Sam's funeral.

"We're John and Agni Johnson. We knew Sam since the day we were born. We grew up playing and dreaming of our futures together. Even when he was promoted to the head of the Institute he had time for us. Sam was a kind, down to earth friend. He always asked us if we needed anything. No matter how busy, Sam remembered his friends." The twins looked at their father and then the crowd. Speaking alternately they said, "Our father, Bubba Johnson has always wanted us to stay out of Roman business. We have always honored our father's wishes. But after this, we can no longer stand idle. We have joined the Institute's military force and we will not rest until we help end this new evil plague of fear, hate and racism. Sam deserved better then to have his friends step aside. We will not." The two young men touched their chests with their arms and in unison saluted Sam's coffin as they shouted, "*Custodes Mundi,* forever.*"*

Last to speak was Sheamus. "I have been ta too many of these here funerals. All were good people. They were people who cared, they was. Sam had a lot on his shoulders. He was o' true believer in ta code. He may well had become o' great one but he was never fully prepared. Though he had the Lads and was taught by John Roman himself, he still needed him. This wouldn't have happened if John were around. Because of this here act, and what we be seein' in reports, I don't think we Lads can handle what's comin.'

So after this here funeral I'll be headen' out. I'll sure as hell find John and bring him back here. We're going ta end this here rebellion...these new...anti-Starling...whatever bunch o' hooligans. These here mutts who think they can destroy ta world. They better start makin' out their wills, because when I get back they'll not only face ta wrath o' me and ta lads but they'll be facin,' *John bloody Roman, himself*!!!!

The crowd let out a roar off approval and started to chant for the next half hour, John Roman, John Roman.

The Lads starting arguing the minute the service was over. As they made their way to the parking lot Sheamus was first to speak, "Well ain't we o' bunch o' wallygobbers? We let someone go waltzin' in and slit ta throat o' ta man we were sworn ta protect. I can just imagine what John would say."

"We wouldn't have to imagine if John had stayed," Bubba said.

"Stay is it? Ta man gave his entire life ta saving ta world. He fought in wars, against evil, he fought for the rights o' ta people all his life. It cost him dearly. Two loves, friends, *his* future, which he never got. How much more did ya want him ta give?" Sheamus asked.

"It was the life he was born to and accepted, Shea," Terry said, "Hell, he checked out the last four years. Wasn't that enough, 'rest.'?"

"Ach ta hell with ya's. Yer never knew true love. None o' ya ever loved like o' true son o' Ireland."

"Shea's right, dad, Terry," John Johnson said.

"John, Agni get your asses back home. This is no place for you," Bubba said.

"You're wrong Dad," Agni said. "We're in. whether you like it or not."

"Is that so? How about I beat your asses all the way home?" Bubba warned.

"You can try. But together we'll kick your ass," John said.

"Dad. We have never disobeyed you. But this time we are. We're twenty eight and know what we're doing. We hoped you'd let us join you. Show us the ropes; tell us where the land mines are. But if you don't want us, we'll go it alone," Agni Johnson said. Bubba's face flushed and he balled his fists.

"Hold on, Bubba darlin'." Sheamus said as he gently put his hand on Bubba's arm. "They're right. It be o' whole lot better ifin they came in with us and we could train them some more. Look after them ya might say. Better than not knowin' where they be."

"He has a point, Bubba," Terry agreed. "Keep them under our wing for a bit. If you think they're safer because they're not with us, you're mistaken. This group knows all our weaknesses. The boys would be in more danger if left alone."

Bubba sighed and said, "Alright. Alright. You can join us. But you better well listen and learn before you go off and try some foolhardy hero shit." Both the boys smiled at each other and shook hands all around.

"Well now that we got that there done, I'm off ta find John. But first I'll be stoppin' ta see that there Archieréas fella."

"Sounds good, Shea. In the meantime me, Bubba and the boys here will try to get more intel on what happened and continue to watch over the Institute for any problems," Terry said.

"Sounds like a plan. Come on sons, I'll give you your first lesson," Bubba said.

"Great dad. What is it," John asked.

"The two of you can clean our offices," Bubba replied.

****

An hour later, Sheamus arrived at Archieréas' house. After passing the gate, then led to Archieréas' home, Sheamus was invited in and taken to Archieréas. Upon entering the large living room, Sheamus was welcomed by Archieréas with a bow, an open left hand and a sweeping of the ground with the right. Sheamus hesitated but remembered what John had taught him and awkwardly replicated the Anaptýsso greeting. "I ugh...hope I didn't mangle that too badly yer lordship?" Sheamus said.

"Not at all, Mr. O'Keefe," Archieréas thought through a translator. Sheamus smiled and noticed a Starling standing next to Archieréas. What surprised him was how much the Starling resembled John Roman. "I don't have ta pleasure of knowin' yer guest, Archieréas, sir."

"I'll introduce myself if you don't mind, my friend?" The Starling said and thought to Archieréas.

"Well I'll be o' bloody Black and Tan, ya can talk and do that there telepathy thin', hey boyo.'?"

"You are correct, Mr. O'Keefe. We Starlings are born telepathic. Among other things."

"The other thin' bein' better than either human or Anaptýsso. And what's with still looking so much like John. I thought the Starlings have been breeding themselves lately? And why are ya all so damn thin? Ya looks like ya need ta eat, mate." The Starling stood six-three with a slim athletic build. With his tan skin, blue eyes and dark hair he did indeed look a lot like John Roman, except for being taller and much slimmer.

"We don't consider it 'better,' but rather different. By the way my name is Invictus R. Moonchild. As you might guess the R. stands for Roman and, yes, I was born on the moon in the great, *regio*. As for looking like the father of our kind, I appreciate the compliment. As for our physical appearance, space had a lot to do with that. Living, breeding, loving, in space shapes the body quite differently than it does if one lives with earth's gravity."

"Yeah, well I guess John was...err..is...o' handsome bloke. Me name be Sheamus O'Keefe. Ta one and only true son o' Ireland." Turning to Archieréas, Sheamus said, "It's nice ta meet yer friend but I've come ta tell ya I'm goin' off ta find, John. Do ya have any ideas that could help me?"

"Yes, I know that's why you came. It is also why I invited Invictus here to speak with you. Shea, you must find John. We believe the very existence of humans and Anaptýsso are at stake," Archieréas thought.

Sheamus looked at Invictus then at Archieréas, "What? Are ya tellin' me you 'star-people' *will* attack, like these fucks say you will?"

"No, Sheamus it….,." Invictus started to say.

"Hey! Boyo.' It be Mr. O'Keefe ta ya till I say different," Sheamus bristled.

"Shea. Please. Invictus is not the enemy. He is here to help," Archieréas thought.

Calming down, Sheamus asked Archieréas, "I apologize. It's been o' stressful few days yer lordship. I apologize ta ya, Invictus. Feel free ta call me, Shea."

"Shea. We believe the Institute and the UGN are slowly being turned into an anti-Starling force. Hard right political appointees are being installed in important positions of power. Your own Roman Institute's executive board has seen major changes since Sam's death," Archieréas thought.

"We are convinced these changes will come in soft, as they declare their only agenda is the safety of everyone. However, as they attain more more power they will eventually want the Starlings, gone," Invictus said.

"Yeah I could see that happenin'." Sheamus turned to Invictus. "Is that when you attack us?"

"Shea. The Starlings despise war. It is a fruitless endeavor. It should be beneath any sentient being's desire. However, ….."

"Here we go. There's always o' however or o' but, whenever the uppity ups want to gloss over some shite they want ta do." Sheamus retorted.

"If you want to put it that way, fine," Invictus said. "We will defend ourselves. We have lives to lead, families, hopes and dreams. The only nightmare we have is we might have to fight the very family who gave us existence. The family of our father, John Roman. It would be the last choice. We know we would win, but the lasting physiological harm to Starlings would be devastating. Our scientists have projected that destroying the very race who created us would cause schisms in our culture. Factions would become more and more hardened to each other. Eventually, within two thousand years there would be civil war and destruction of the Starlings. So you see, war with earth is a temporary fix, and a bad one at that. In the end it would mean our destruction also. Our desire is to explore the heavens and to honor the family of our creator, John Roman. It is written in our constitution, our way of life, from the time we could read as children we are taught to honor our forefathers. We want to protect and see all Humýsso thrive. There are no winners in war; only death. So we are with you, Shea, and all Humýsso who want to live in peace and harmony."

"Ok. Then help me find, John. He's ta key. The others will follow John and rid us all of the anti-Starling threat," Sheamus said.

"The latest information we have if that he was in your neck of the woods, Shea," Archieréas thought.

"Ya mean ta ole country, do ya?"

"Yes indeed, the ole country," Archieréas smiled.

"We suggest you take John and Agni Johnson," Invictus said.

"Why would I want ta take them young boys? They still need some trainin' and Bubba would never go for it."

"If our sources are right, the boys could be in danger here. With you gone and only Terry and Bubba here, the anti-Starling forces will make their move. They'll go down the list, a purge, if you like. Something this kind of coup always winds up having. Take them with you, Shea. Teach them on the way and keep them safe. When you and John return, you will need them," Archieréas counseled.

"Well if that be ta case, ta boys and me be havin' ta sneak out in ta middle o' ta night. I'm sure I'll be in for o' beatin' by me dear friend, Bubba when I get back."

"What's a small beating between friends when it means saving the world?" Archieréas smiled.

Sheamus shook Invictus and Archieréas' hand and then left. He met the boys that night and they all agreed to the plan. Sheamus decided to take Bubba out for a drink in order for John and Agni to pack. The three travelers were to meet at midnight.

****

At seven, Sheamus and Bubba started to drink as they watched the sunset at the cabin John left them. "Ahh now. I've never seen o' more beautiful sight, exceptin' o' course in ta finest land on earth, me Ireland," Sheamus said as he put the bottle of Baileys whiskey to his lips.

"*Your* Ireland? What about all the other people who live there?" Bubba said as he drank.

"Blah. I be ta only true son o' Ireland, I am. The others, all just imitators they is."

"You always...hic...were a...selfeeeish..selfish...son of a...bitch," Bubba slurred his words as he drank down another mouthful of whiskey.

"Nah, me friend. How can ya say that about Sheamus O'Keefe? Never was there such o' man as shared his-self so generously with ta world now." The two friends drank until near midnight, sharing stories and memories of the past. Sheamus heard a twig snap in the woods and looked up to see the boys. He put his finger to his lips and pointed at Bubba. John and Agni froze.

"What say we down one last big shot o' nature's honey, me Baileys here, and call it o' night? Here's ta John Roman, ta best man I know."

Bubba stood up on wobbly legs and toasted, "To Jooohn...hic...Ro...hic..Roman." Finishing the near half full bottle, Bubba looked at Sheamus, then the moon, and promptly passed out cold. Sheamus and the boys gently put him to bed. "I'll give ya some time with yer Da," Sheamus said as he stepped outside.

Kneeling by his bed the boys held their fathers hand as they put a letter* on his pillow. "We left you a letter Dad. It will explain everything. We love you," They whispered.

*"To Mom and Dad. Please don't be mad at Shea or us. We promise to be careful but we must do this. Sam was our friend and you taught us to always care about family and friends. The world needs us, Dad. We are part of what's happening. We can't stand by and let others risk their lives. We love you both. Kiss mom for us."

Chapter Ten

The Search for John Begins

By the time Bubba awoke, Sheamus and the boys were miles away. Little did John or Agni Johnson know they would never see their father alive again. The first stop on their journey to find John was Uli wa Liánhé. Sheamus showed the two young men the cave where Raiden avenged his sister, Aimi. It was the beginning of a near year-long search for John. Along the way, Sheamus regaled John and Agni with tales of the Lads and John Roman. Sheamus used every opportunity to further train the two young men in combat, tactics, weapons and the rare ability to see ahead of one's opponent. Despite Sheamus' braggadocios tales of heroism, he did teach the young men, the value of honor, patience, empathy and courage. The three became close friends, and Sheamus was not only a mentor, but a father-figure as well. Their journey was filled with companionship, adventure and laughter.

Back home, however, there was little to laugh about. After awaking from his drunken stupor and finding his sons gone, Bubba was determined to find them. The next day Bubba was packing when Kimiko and Terry, stopped him. "Dear husband. Where do you intend to start looking for our sons. Did you not read the letter? This is something they must do. Besides, they are with Shea. No one could protect them better."

"She's right, Bubba. Look, we need John back here. Things at the Institute and the UGN are turning sour. Frank Langdon is going to be elected chancellor of the UGN. You don't get anyone more anti-Starling. In the meantime the Institute executive board is slowly being replaced by pro Langdon supporters. I need someone here I can trust, Bubba. At least until Shea and your boys come back with John. Then you can kick Shea's ass," Terry laughed.

"Nothing to laugh at, Terry. I'm going to do a lot more than kick Shea's ass," Bubba said as he slammed his suitcase shut. "All right. But while I stay here and help I need you to find out where my boys are and if they're safe."

"It's a deal, my friend."

****

Eight months after their search started, Sheamus and the boys landed at the Michael Collins airport, in what was old Ireland. Now part of the Nation of Europa, many residents of this green island still used Gaelic as their first language and thought of their home as Ireland. Though not illegal, the idea of Ireland as separate from Europa was frowned upon as reactionary. The school books never called the island Ireland except as an historical reference. It was late afternoon when the fellas stopped at the *Erin go Bragh* pub in New Dublin. Located at the northern end of the island after the ice melted,

New Dublin had become the center of tourism, intrigue and secession talk. As Sheamus and the boys sat down at a table, a beautiful red headed lass came up to take their order.

"*Dia Duit.* What ya be having, lads?"

Sheamus knew the Gaelic greeting meant this was a secessionist pub.

"*Dia Duit* yerself, lass." The girl gave a knowing smile.

"Well now young lady. Seein' as how we have just come in from ta cold, we be startin' with o' shot each o' Bailey's Irish whiskey and o' few pints o' ya best draft,"

"Fine. Ya lads wantin' anythin' ta eat now?"

"What I be wantin' is yer name, me lovely," Sheamus said.

"Easy there, grandpa. Me name is Brigid and that's all ya get."

"Well, can *we* order?" John asked.

Bending over the table, Brigid sultry voice cooed, "Ya lads can order anything ya want. Even somethin' that may not be on ta menu."

Looking at each other, Agni turned to Brigid and said, "That's...ahh...great ba...but for now can we have three orders of the beef stew?" Agni asked.

"And...ugh...if my brother isn't interested, I would love to discuss the off menu items later," John added.

"Well ain't ya ta cheeky one, now? What be yer name, me handsome one?" Brigid asked.

"Excuse me, but we are twins. He can't be handsome with…"

Under the table, Sheamus kicked Agni's foot and whispered, "Shh, son. Looks ain't ta only thin' which turns o' woman's head, lad."

As Brigid left to get the guys their food Sheamus told the twins about a lead he had.

"See here boys. I got this friend who has assured me he can point us in ta right direction. He says o' man has been comein' down from ta hills for o' year now, once o' month. The man stops at two places. The 'Jimmy Barnes Supply Depot' and this here pub. Me friend says the man gets o' pint and two shots o' Baileys whiskey, downs em as he drinks his pint, then leaves o' tip and off he goes. Never says o' word ta anyone."

"Did he say what the man looked like?" Do you trust him, Shea?" Agni asked

"Well, I'll put it this way, lad. I'd loan him o' fiver but wouldn't count on it bein' returned."

Chapter Eleven

Dangerous Times

As Sheamus and the boys continued their search for John Roman problems in Tsalaki were getting worse. Tanach had been arrested for the murder of Sam Roman. But after a lengthy court battle, she was acquitted for lack of evidence. Many of the witnesses who claimed she was there recanted their stories. Tanach, on the other hand, provided ample witnesses who said she was with them that night. Many of her alibi witnesses were powerful people. That, along with all DNA evidence mysteriously disappearing, left the judge with no other choice but to dismiss.

Tanach's public image team got to work, and after constant bombardment on social media and other outlets, Tanach soon became an icon of feminism and victim-blaming. In the end, Tanach got so brazen she began suggesting, if she did kill Sam, it would have been in self-defense from an attack by a sex crazed man.

So in this new world view, the man who was murdered became the villain, Starlings became a threat for being a peaceful species, and racism became all right, if it meant defending human and Anaptýsso views of their superiority. More and more politicians, who wanted the Starlings gone, were voted into office. More of the pro-Starling people were called traitors. The military was also slowly transforming from a defensive to an offensive arm of Nations. Eight months to the day since Sheamus left, now, "General" Terry Mallory, whose clearance had been getting cut down month by month, was arrested on charges of sedition. Bubba went to see Terry at the Tsalaki military prison where he was being held.

In a courtyard the two men talked about the future. "I pulled some of my last strings to get us this area. Everything inside is bugged. This may well be the final time I get to talk to you, Bubba," Terry said.

"I don't get it, man. No trial, no bond, just throw you in here? What's happening to our democracy, Terry?"

"We got too complacent, my friend. Thought we were invulnerable to this type of insurrection. It was a slow burn. Bit by bit. I believe these traitors are ready for the final step. A full complete dictatorial take over of at least four nations: Tsalaki, Mama Ocllo, Acharya and maybe Taka."

"Taka!! Archieréas would never let that happen," Bubba said.

"Not while he was alive he wouldn't," Terry replied.

"You think they plan to kill Archieréas? Are they that powerful? What about the Anaptýsso? You really think they would back the anti-Starling group if Archieréas were assassinated?"

"Bubba, they murdered Sam fucking Roman. In his own house. Not only did they get away with it, but some consider Tanach and her acolytes' heroes. If they have enough Anaptýsso in the right places, and a hold on the media, I'm sure they could pull it off. The Anaptýsso are like any other species. If they think their lives are threatened, they will react. For years, this notion that the Starlings are just waiting to take over the earth and make slaves of humans and Anaptýsso has been pounded into the heads of both groups by, politicians, *True News* and the rest of Lenny Murtock's outlets and all those who copy his racist, hateful fueled lies and disinformation rhetoric."

"How can we protect, or at least warn, Archieréas?"

"I can't do anything from here. So it's up to you. Get to Archieréas. Tell him what's going on."

Terry then cupped his hands around his mouth in case anyone was watching his lips.

"Go to 100 Atwells Avenue. Apartment 1110. Knock three times, stop, then two quick taps. An old woman will open the door. Tell her, 'Terry the T sent you'. She should answer back, 'Hope he's alright since he never calls his mother'. The woman will hand you a letter with a code which you can use once you have the f-drives. She knows nothing about the f-drives just the letter. So after she gives you the letter, tell her to go downstairs and wait. We kept the operative on a need to know basis. The woman is a talker. We couldn't trust her with everything. Go to the back bedroom and underneath the leg of the top right bedpost you'll find the bottom of the leg hollow. Unscrew the cap and there will be two f-drives. They're no bigger than a ten unit GMU so be careful. Bring those to

Archieréas. If what's on those f-drives doesn't convince him nothing will."

At that very moment a voice came over the loudspeaker, "Mallory! Time's up, now."

"Bubba looked at Terry as three guards started walking toward them. "Don't worry, Terry. I'll get the stuff to Archieréas."

The guard punished Bubba aside and cuffed Terry dragging him back to his cell. As they did he shouted to Bubba, "Remember, if anything happens to me in here it wasn't suicide."

****

Later that day, making sure he was not followed, Bubba made his way to the address Terry had given him. Entering Sister Domina's home for the elderly, he was soon at the door to apartment 1110. Knocking just as Terry instructed him to, Bubba was soon greeted by. "Hello," from an old woman.

"Terry the T sent me," Bubba replied.

"'Hope he's alright since he never calls his mother,'" the old woman said, as she invited Bubba in. once again Bubba's gut was telling him to be careful. Something just didn't feel right. As he stood in the living room, the old woman asked, "My name is Myrtle, what's yours?"

"Bubba, ma'am. If you knew the code then you must know why I'm here."

"Oh yes. Please come in and find what you need. Would you like something to drink?"

"No, ma'am. Why did you say, 'find what I need'?"

"Excuse me?"

"Yeah., and where's the letter?"

At that second, the woman sprung at Bubba. Dodging the attack, Bubba grabbed the woman and flipped her to the ground. A swift kick to her face knocked the old lady out.

As he was securing the "woman," Bubba realized it was no woman at all but a man wearing a disguise. Awakening his attacker, Bubba asked, "So. Who are you? Who do you work for? You know all the questions I'm going to ask. You don't have any cyanide in your mouth, so no checking out."

Bubba pulled a knife from the kitchen drawer and made his way to the man. "I just kicked someone I thought was a woman in the face. If you think this will go easy, think again."

"Look, pal. I'm just a hired hand. I don't know shit….ahhhhhh..fuck!!!" The man screamed as Bubba stabbed the man's leg with the knife and twisted it.

"Don't worry *pal*. I know where the arteries are. You won't bleed out," Bubba smiled.

"Shit!! Come on man. I'm just a hired….motherfucker…." The man yelled as Bubba twisted the knife again.

"Where's the woman who was supposed to be here?" Bubba asked'

"Look, man. You don't....Wait...wait," The man said, as Bubba started to move toward the knife.

"She's in the closet."

Bubba opened the closet door and saw the dead woman. "You had to murder an old woman?

"Look man, you just don't realize she never shut up. She never stopped talking. Hell, she gave you guys up without me asking her. The fuck just wouldn't shut up and half the time she just kept repeating the same shit over and over again. I couldn't take it anymore," The man said.

"Let me guess. After I found what I came here for, you were going to kill me," Bubba asked.

"Hey man. You know the deal. It's what we do. Nothing personal."

Bubba said, "I'll be right back, don't go anywhere."

Bubba went to the bedroom and found the f-drives. He then went back to the man in the chair.

"You see this? It's what you killed the old lady for and what you were gong to kill me for."

"Yeah, I get it. But like I said, nothing personal, man"

Bubba then looked at the man's eyes and whispered, "Nothing personal, man." as he put the knife through the man's heart.

****

That night Bubba talked with Kimiko about what Terry had told him.

"Sweetheart, I have to do this. You know that, right?"

"Of course my dear." Kimiko looked down at their album pictures and said to Bubba, "My love, we have been so blessed. So lucky. Look at our boys. We've known friends like Cass and John. We have had over twenty years together. The world needs us now. If it means we might have to give up our lives to make everyone's sons and daughters safe, then we must try. We can't sit idly or fearfully on the sidelines."

"Alright. I'm glad you said that. I've always known you had more courage then me, especially when it came to our boys. I wanted to keep them in a cocoon, so nothing could ever hurt them. But you knew they had to fly on their own. I'm going to see Archieréas. I've made copies of these," Bubba said as he handed Kimiko two f-drives. You need to go to Uli wa Liánhé. You'll be safe there. When…"

"I'm not going to run and hide. I just told…"

"No. No my darling. This isn't about hiding. In fact if Tanach and her bunch think you have these, your life will be in great danger. No my love. This is not hiding. It's making sure these don't get buried. Take them to Akemi Kameyama. She is Aimi's sister. The family respects John and the Institute. These will be safe with them."

"Very well. When do we go?"

"Tonight. As soon as possible. Pack light and let's go."

"Tonight! You think it's that dangerous to stay here until tomorrow?"

"Absolutely. They know I met with Terry today. I wouldn't put it past them to send people here to kill us. I have a private jet which will take you directly to the Kameyama family's personal airport. They will meet you there."

Kimiko and Bubba threw together some essentials and then met in the living room.

"What about you? Kimiko said with a worried frown.

"I'm going to make my way on foot to Archieréas. I wouldn't put it pass them to have the car or my watch bugged. Bubba took off his T-50 and smashed it with his booted heel. Here, take a couple of these burner phones. Only use then if it's an emergency. After I see Archieréas I'll call you."

At that moment a car horn sounded outside. "That's Jerry. He'll take you to the plane. Now give me a kiss and I'll see you when this is over."

After Kimiko was safely away, Bubba turned and looked at the house he had lived in with Kimiko for nearly twenty years. The home where he had raised his sons. Something in his gut said he would never return and he was right.

****

The next morning Bubba jumped over the wall of Principium. He stealthily made his way to Archieréas' to the front door. Three Makete and a human came out of seemingly nowhere and surrounded him. "Hello Mr. Johnson. My name is Germat. I am Archieréas aide. He has been monitoring you since you came over the wall, Mr. Johnson. Please follow us. Archieréas is eager to speak with you."

Entering Archieréas' home, the three Makete stopped at the door. Following Germat into the living room, Bubba was impressed by its decor and style.

"Would you like something to drink or eat, Mr. Johnson?" Germat asked.

"Ahh...yeah, as a matter of fact. I'm pretty dry and tired after spending the night getting here on foot. I'll have some water and anything with caffeine or add-up. Ehh...also, please just, Bubba is fine."

"Very well...Bubba. We keep neither caffeine or add-up but we do make our own 'wake-up juice' you might say. I'm sure you will find it refreshing."

"Sounds good to me, Germat."

Returning quickly, Germat sat the two drinks down along with some food. "I took it upon myself to offer you this, Bubba. They will revive your body and they taste good. I don't know how familiar your are with Anaptýsso food but these are a sampling of some of their favorite meals."

Bubba was very hungry so he hesitantly tried a piece and instantly found it wonderful. He then started to try all the different choices until he had his fill.

"'Wow. I must seem like a real pig. But I'll tell you man. Where has this stuff been all my life? It all tastes so good."

"It has been here all the time. I also don't find it offensive. I know you must be hungry and I cooked it all so it makes me proud you like it. I am always happy when I see humans try Anaptýsso food for the first time. I have learned so much from them. The Anaptýsso seem to bring an extra flavor not only to their food, but to fashion, art, philosophy and life itself. Sort of 'human point 2.0' you might say."

"Then what would Starlings be? 'Anaptýsso point 4.0'?"

Germat seemed to reflect on this and then said, "Maybe. But would that be a bad thing? As a human I have found the Anaptýsso way of living exhilarating. I would hope I will find the Starling way of life even more exalting. The problem is, we humans and Anaptýsso share this world. When was the last time you met a Starling? They have inherited the universe. They don't seem to care about this world anymore. They have no major cities here on earth. Only a few private homes in major Nation cities. They do have representation but there is no trade, no exchange of ideas, no plans for us in their world. We seem, to many, to have been left behind."

"Yeah. I can see that. But they have no major cities because they can't take earth's gravity. It's uncomfortable for them. Those few homes you talk about house the Starling representatives to those perspective Nations. Imagine how much dedication that takes to give up a life among the stars just to keep channels open between species? As far as trade. No. they have none yet because so far they have given us all the discoveries they have found, for free. Buy the way, you got anymore of this green stuff?"

"It's called 'almosta' and yes, we do. I'll be right back."

"Yeah and some more of this...ahh..wake-up juice."

"That's called, 'litoma.' we have several flavors. Would you like a different one?" Germat said as he was walking to the kitchen.

"No. No, this is fine, thank you." Bubba took the last bite of the green meat and thought, "Almosta,,hey. Christ I, almosta, swallowed my tongue eating this, it's so good."

Before Germat returned, Archieréas entered the room with his translator. "I am so glad you like our food Bubba."

Standing up Bubba said, "Hell you scared me there, Archieréas. But yeah...yes, I loved it. But I'm here for more important matters."

"We both are, Bubba," Germat said as he reentered with the almosta.

"Wait...what's going…" Bubba stammered.

"Please sit, Bubba. We haven't talked since the end of the war." Archieréas said through his translator.

A little embarrassed Bubba replied.
"Well...ahh...yeah...you're right. It's just that...well kids and ahh...you know...ahhh."

"Please. Please, don't worry. I completely understand. After a war many who were and still are friends drift. For some it's a matter of not wanting to relive memories. But we are friends, I assure you Bubba."

"Yeah, that works for me, Archieréas." Turning to Germat, Bubba said, "I'm guessing you're not just a chef or aide. All that chit-chat before was feeling me out." Turning back to Archieréas, "Were you listening the whole time?"

"I must confess, I was," Archieréas' translator said.

"My friend, we can let your translator go now that I'm here. Less confusing," Germat said to Archieréas.

"You are right," Archieréas thought and then dismissed his man.

As Bubba looked back at Germat, Germat continued, "Your guess is right, Bubba. I am the leader of the human side of this equation. We are working hard to overthrow the anti-Starling faction. Who, I am afraid to say, is growing in strength."

"Tell me about it. General Terry Mallory has been arrested and put in prison. The bad guys are looking for me. I'm sure it's not to give me a medal or birthday card. I sent Kimiko away where she will be safe and I came here to deliver you these." Bubba handed the two f-drives to Germat.

"They contain everything Terry had on these people and Anaptýsso. Many of the names on these are the heads of the anti-Starling faction. They are also in powerful positions." Looking at Germat, Bubba continued, "I'm afraid your high opinion of the Anaptýsso may take a beating, Germat. Yours also, Archieréas. Seems more than a few of the Anaptýsso, especially the Makete are on the anti-Starling side."

Both Archieréas and Germat seemed frustrated and ashamed. "Yes. You are right, my friend. It seems many of our young Makete, with no outlet for their aggression have turned to sex as a release. Sex with humans. Being offered by Tanach's underground group 'Honor the Makete.' It's just a sex cult disguised as a Makete support group. I fear many of our young Makete have fallen under Tanach's spell." Archieréas through Germat.

"Yeah...well it's not just your young. There are high level Anaptýsso names on these," Bubba challenged.

Even more frustrated, Archieréas said through Germat, "You are right. It is my and the Anaptýsso's great shame. Fear, Bubba. Fear of the unknown. Just as the Anaptýsso were feared even after the war, even after our contributions to our shared society, we were still feared by humans. Now humans and Anaptýsso have what they consider a common enemy. The Starlings. So that fear of the, 'Other,' which seems have always infected the human psyche now infects many Anaptýsso. They fear the Starlings, Bubba. Simple as that."

"Sure and what happens *if* the Starlings are destroyed? I'll tell you what. The humans, led by the likes of Tanach Roman, will turn on the Anaptýsso and wipe you out. That's a guarantee." Turning to Germat, Bubba yelled, "So why don't your so called, enlightened Anaptýsso see that, Germat?"

"I'm afraid the *seeming* threat in front of them has blinded their eyes to their true enemy," Germat replied.

"Well we better do something besides standing around moaning about the loss of Anaptýsso honor. Do either of you have any suggestions?" Bubba asked.

"We can hope the information in these f-drives will expose what's really happening. We still are in touch with media outlets, who will broadcast this type of news. We also know people in the political and military sectors who need just this type of evidence to be able to stop these traitors," Germat said.

"We will get this out to everyone tomorrow. We'll make copies and send them to all the Nations. People and Anaptýsso will respond. It's not too late. I promise, Bubba," Archieréas said through Germat.

"Ok, then. In the mean time I'm going to be with Kimiko. I'll talk to you both later. And...ugh... Archieréas...I..ugh promise not to stay away for so long again."

Archieréas bowed and said through Germat, "I hope you and Kimiko stay safe and visit often, my friend."

"We both do,"Germat added. As he walked Bubba to the door Germat asked, "Where is Kimiko? Are you sure she is safe? She would be very well protected here, you know."

"Thank you. But I'm happy where she is."

"Does she have copies of the f-drive?" Germat asked.

Bubba's gut was starting to turn. "Why would you want to know if she had f-drives? Because she doesn't."

"Ahh. You see I don't believe you would just have a single copy of these, Bubba. You're far too smart."

"Let me talk to Archieréas again. I don't like these questions you're asking me," Bubba said.

"I'm afraid it's too late for that, Mr. Johnson." Suddenly the door burst open and a dozen humans and Makete wrestled Bubba to the floor. They then brought him into the living room where Archieréas still was.

"What is the meaning of this?" Archieréas thought through his translator.

"Shut the fuck up, Archieréas," Tanach shouted as she entered the room.

"Germat. You have betrayed us." Tanach then shot Archieréas' translator.

"I told you to shut up. Now, Bubba my dark-colored boy, does Kimiko have copies? Look, I'm going to have her and you killed no matter what. You just have to decide whether her death will be quick, or a long, painful, drawn out process."

"How could you do this after we shared so much for all these years, Germat?" Archieréas thought.

"I saw who was going to win, my friend. Plus I really don't like the Starlings," Germat answered. Suddenly Germat grabbed his head in agony and fell to his knees.

"AHHHHH!!! Get out of my head," Germat shouted.

As Tanach yelled for her henchmen to stop Archieréas from hurting Germat, Bubba took the opportunity to head butt Tanach directly in her face, breaking her nose and knocking her to the ground. He then shoved two humans and grabbed one of their guns.

Shooting and wounding three Makete, Bubba ran for the door, sprinted outside and went out over the wall. In the living room, Germat gave one last painful yell and collapsed dead on the floor.

"Didn't share that with you *proditor,* Archieréas thought to himself.

Tanach turned to Archieréas holding a towel against her face as she tried to stop the bleeding coming from her damaged nose.

"Yoaa...mottherfuccors. Thaaath cocooocka sucur broke my fuckiiin noosee."

Moving directly within an inch of Archieréas face, Tanach said. "Doeess...Kiiehmiehko have coopiees?" As Archieréas stood there smiling, Tanach got more enraged. One of the men with her said, "He can't answer. You killed the translator."

Tanach screamed, "AHHH!!" Then she stabbed the man in his neck with her Starling ceremonial knife. "Anyee wone elsss?" After stopping the bleeding, Tanach stuffed two pieces of toilet paper up her nostrils. "Get someone in here who can..," Tanach was about to say when a man raised his hand and said, "I can translate."

"Well get to it. Ask him where Bubba is going and if Kimiko has any copies."

After the man thought Tanach's words. Archieréas told him to stop. "You need only translate my thoughts to her. I can hear her."

"Yes, your reverence," The man thought.

"What is your name?" Archieréas asked.

"It is Rodger Samuel, your reverence."

"Are you not afraid I will do to you what I did to Germat?"

"If that is your wish. I only joined them tonight because I knew they were coming here. To be before you is the honor of my life. To die by your hand would complete me. You should know they are going to kill you," Rodgers warned.

"Yes. It is my time."

"Hey!!! You two start saying something I can hear or you'll both be dead. Are there any copies?"

"Tell her yes," Archieréas thought.

"Yes." Rodger repeated.

"Well!! You fuckers, where are they?"

Archieréas thought and Rodgers asked him, "Are you sure?"

Archieréas nodded. Rodgers turned to Tanach and said, "The copies are up your twat, bitch."

Tanach became so enraged she grabbed a machine gun from one of the intruders and stared to empty the clip at Archieréas. In the second before his death Archieréas put his hands on Samuel's head and a feeling of utter bliss went through the man's mind.

Looking to the heavens and smiling, Archieréas' last thought was, "We ascend my friend."

"Fuck!!!" Was all Tanach could say after killing Archieréas. Turning to her cohorts she yelled,

"Find that black fucker NOW!!!"

Bubba had been running for what seemed an hour and he was panting heavily. Coming to a large clearing in an open field he fell to the ground. Looking up at the stars he thought of Kimiko, his sons, John and the rest of the Lads. His life played out before him as his chest seized up. Talking to the universe he thought, "Please keep Kimiko safe. Please don't let anything bad happen to my boys. Help John and that damn Irishman win this battle."

Feeling the life flow out of him as his heart stopped, Bubba stared at the moon and infinite starlight in the sky and thought, "Man. Been a hell of a ride."

Chapter Twelve

The Search Ends

After leaving the *Erin go Bragh* pub, Sheamus suggested they stake out the Jimmy Barnes Supply Depot.

"Christ Shea, your friend said the guy only comes about once a month," Agni lamented. "are we going to wait here for a month?"

"Nay, fellas. See that there roomin' house across ta street? I got us o' month's lease. We keep o' round ta clock watch on that there store. Ya see, me friend also told this here fellow Irishman, that ta man was here three weeks ago. Which means we should only have ta wait o' wee bit. Besides ifin he only *comes* once o' month, he must be o' real impatient fella," Sheamus quipped, laughing heartily at his own joke.

John turned to his brother Agni and said, "If that's any indication of what we have to look forward to with the three of us in that room, god help us." Agni nodded his head in affirmation and grinned from ear to ear. The three men entered their single room and realized there was only one bed.

"Ehhh, excuse me Shea. But how are the three of us going to sleep in a single bed?" Agni asked.

Scratching his head as he took his tam off, Sheamus jumped on the small bed and said, "Well, boys I can tell ya it's quite comfortable. Now look. It was all I could afford for o' month lease. We all aren't gonna sleep at at same time anyway, lads. One of us has ta keep watch. The other two can easily share this here bed. Why when I were o' wee lad we slept five of us in o' bed half this size. Now stop bein' such gobbolywonks. I'll take ta first watch and the two of ya can take yerselves o' nap."

Sighing loudly John said, "Alright, fine but where's the bathroom?"

"Oh that be right down ta hallway at at far end, lad," Sheamus replied.

"Christ." John said as he made his way to the toilet. When he got there and opened the door he almost wretched. The room was filthy. The floor, sink and bathtub looked as if they hadn't been cleaned in weeks. The toilet still had crap in it. John held his nose and flushed the floating turd-filled bowl. After relieving himself, John returned to the room and told Sheamus what he had encountered.

Half asleep by now, Sheamus said, "There ya go again, complainin'. Why in my day, we didn't even have o' pot ta piss in. We had ta go out inta the cold whenever we had to do our business. We used corn husks ta wipe our arse. Hell lad, ya got it good here. Just keep o' positive attitude, like yer uncle Shea."

Two days later at midday, John J. saw a man with a full head of hair and a bushy beard walk into the, Jimmy Barnes Supply

Depot. "Hey. Hey, uncle Shea. Wake up," John J. said as he shook Sheamus.

"Easy, easy, lad. Ya woke me out of o' dream. I was courtin' that there lovely lass from across ta street. What was the dear girl's name?"

"Never mind that, I just saw a guy who might be John." Sheamus bolted out of his stupor and went to the window. "Where? Where, mate?"

"He went into the Depot. About two minutes ago."

"Aright, lad. Make sure he doesn't leave without ya seein' where he goes. I got ta release this here bladder o' mine. Wake yer brother and tell him ta get dressed."

Returning from the loo, Sheamus went to the window. "Any sign of ta fella?"

"No. not yet, uncle Shea," John J. said.

"Alright then. Agni. If that guy don't come out in o' minute or two I want y…"

"Wait," John J. whispered. "There he is. He's going into the *Erin go Bragh*."

Sheamus looked out at the bearded man and in a barely audible voice said, "Saint Micheal, shut these Irish eyes forever if what I be seein isn't John fuckin' Roman himself."

With that Sheamus jumped up, ran down the stairs and across the street. The boys scrambled to catch up with their uncle. At the entrance to the *Erin go Bragh*, Sheamus saw the man sitting at the pub's last stool, facing the door. Sheamus walked slowly in and as

John looked up he downed a shot of Bailey's whiskey followed by a swig from his pint. He then stood watching Sheamus walk toward him.

"Barkeep, give us what that man is havin and refill his, will ya now?"

As Sheamus stood facing John, the two men looked into each others eyes for what seemed like an eternity. John J. and Agni J. froze in place looking at both men, not knowing what was going to happen.

"Is it truly John I be lookin' at, yer dirty heathen' ya?"

With the tiniest of smiles John answered, "It's me, you Irish bastard."

The two then embraced in a tight hug that lasted almost too long. Breaking the bro-hug, the two patted each other on the back and then sat.

"These two must be John and Agni Johnson," John asked.

"Aye, they be those fellas."

"Grown up quite a bit I see. I'm surprised your father let you go anywhere with this guy."

"Well ta two boys didn't give him much choice," Sheamus laughed.

John grew silent and then said, "This can't be a 'how-you-doing-call', Shea. Why are you here?"

"John, ya got ta come back. Ta whole place be goin' ta hell. These anti-Starlin' people and some Anaptýsso I might be addin' are about ta start o' war that at best will exterminate the Starlin's and eventually the Anaptýsso. But me guess is, ifin' these idiots start somethin' with the Starlin's, they is goin' ta get all of ta earth's inhabitants killed."

"I think you're right on that part, Shea. Unless the anti-Starling bunch has some kind of secret weapon, I think the Starlings would wipe them out in a war."

"What ya be sayin, John? Ya don't care what happens ta innocent people?"

"Yeah...well...maybe the humans need to be wiped out. As far as innocence goes, humans haven't done a very good job of caring for each other or this planet. Everything has its time, Shea. This could be humanity's time to pay up."

"I know ya had some losses in yer life, John. But tellin' ta whole world ta fuck off ain't like ta man I knew. And what ya mean by, 'humans' and 'them'? In case ya fergot, John, yer human,"Sheamus said.

Looking directly at Sheamus John said, "There's where you're wrong, Shea. I'm not human."

"What kind o' talk is that? Yer was born human and yer still are. Doesn't matter if some virus or foreign blood got inta ya. Yer still human, John. Ya got ta come back and help, John. The world needs ya."

"Shea, even if I wanted to help, I'm eighty-five for Christ's sake."

"Don't give me that there bullshit. Hell, ya look fifty and besides, like ya said, life expectancy is a hundred and ten these days. And that's just for hu..." Sheamus caught himself."

John smiled, "For humans? You're right. And because I'm *not* human, I was told by Cass that my life expectancy was a hundred and forty. So, great for me. I get to live another fifty plus years without Cass and...." John suddenly flew off his stool as Sheamus punched him right in the face.

"Get up yer self-pityin' fool. Get up. I'm gonna beat ta whinin'" out ya."

As John stood, he wiped his bloody mouth, smiled and said, "I think you've been waiting to do that for a long time, my friend."

Taking a boxer's stance, Sheamus started moving around John saying, "Come on yer blubbery sad sack ya. Put'em up. This here is goin' ta be a valuable lesson I'll be given' ya, Johnny boy."

"Shea, I don't want to figh..." Before John could finish his sentence he was down on the floor again.

"Come on. Get up, yer piece o' shite."

From the floor John said, "I'll not fight you, Shea. So I'm going to stay on the floor."

"Nay. That won't save ya, yer cowardly gollywob." Sheamus moved to pick John up and hit him again when suddenly the lights went out and Sheamus fell to the floor. When he awoke, he found his arms pinned to his side by a set of long legs. Looking up, his eyes saw a shaved vagina covered by a short skirt, kneeling over his face. The person then got up and John held his hand out to help him off the floor. When Sheamus eventually got to his feet he looked at the woman who had cold-cocked him.

"Shea, you remember, Apolla,." John smiled.

"Aye, mate. How could I forget that quiff? Well lass, ya certainly haven't changed much."

"Clean living and a lot of plastic," Apolla said.

"I Thought yer was runnin' ta Outlands, darlin'."

"Yeah. Got too boring. I left and went looking for him," Apolla said nodding toward John. "I knew Cass was gone so I figured maybe he needed some place warm to rest that pole between his legs."

"Christ almighty, John. It seems anyone can find ya. What kind o' hideout ya got goin' here?"

"Really? Well it took you eight months. Besides, I still have a lot of people who keep me informed. I know who's doing what to whom and who's trying to find me."

"So ya knew we was lookin' for ya for eight months but did nothin,' boyo'? When did she get here?"

"I gave Apolla here a ping a couple of years ago," John said as he downed his second shot and sighed, "A man gets lonely, Shea. It's nice to feel another's warmth on cold nights."

"That's right. I've been waiting for my *lyubovnik* to call for me. I knew my time would come," Apolla said as she put her arms around John and smiled. "We are together now. So if you ever try to hurt him, I'll kill you."

"Don't worry, lass. It was just o' misunderstandin'," Sheamus said angrily, slamming his shot glass down on the table. "I thought I found John Roman but it was just an impostor. Come on, lads. Let's get back home. We got o' war ta win." As Sheamus and the boys started to walk out he turned to John. "Oh ya high and mighty good fer nothin'. These here are Bubba Johnson's son's. The lads who thought ya was o' hero. Take o' look fellas. That there used ta be me friend."

Sheamus and the boys left and John sat on his stool for a while. He ordered another shot and drank it.

"Fuck them *lyubovnik*. You don't need that mess anymore. In the end, they won't be satisfied until you give them your life," Apolla said as she stroked John's hair.

John left the pub and saw Sheamus and the lads walking down the street. "Hey!!!" John yelled as he strode toward Sheamus. Getting within two feet of his friend, John hauled off and punched Sheamus in the face, sending him to the ground. John J. and Agni J. went to grab John but he quickly flipped both boys to the ground. Standing over Sheamus, John said, "Come on get up."

"What? Ya gonna hit me again cause I told ta truth?"

"No, Shea," John answered as he held out his hand. "The first whack you gave me I deserved. This punch was for the second shot you hit me with. Now we're even."

Standing up, Sheamus looked at John with love. "Does this here mean me old friend has returned?"

"Yeah, you old Irish rogue. Come on. Let's go to my place and we'll talk tactics."

Turning to Apolla, John said, "This isn't your fight. If you want out, I understand."

"Fuck you my *lyubovnik*," Apolla said as she hugged John tightly. "You are my *lyubovnik*. Forever. Where you go I go."

John then shook the boy's hands saying, "Your father is a good man. I'll be happy to see him and your mother again. As far as me flipping you there, we're going to have to work on your training a bit."

"Oh that's alright, sir," John J. said. "Yeah, it was an honor getting floored by you," Agni J. added.

"Ok. But what we might have to do later will leave no time for hero worship or hesitation. You will need to act decisively and fast," John warned.

"Yes, sir," The two men said in unison.

"Christ, Mary and bloody Joseph. Them two ain't called me 'sir' in eight months. But here comes John Roman and suddenly they be respectin'…"

Everyone laughed, and then followed John.

As everyone exited the pub they saw five men and as many Makete waiting outside the pub.

"I think you've been followed, Shea," John smiled.

"Yea, well if ya had let me know where ya been hidin' this here old fool wouldn't have been so clumsy."

"Fuck that, keep those two children safe," Apolla said pointing to the boys, "This bunch is just a warm up before I have breakfast." With that, Apolla tore into the men, killing two with one swipe of her blade. Sheamus took out both his combat knife and switchblade, making quick work of three more men. John drew his pistol, loaded with explosive ammo, and shot four of the Makete killing them instantly. John J. and Agni J. sped through the rest of the bad guys like two dancers. Spinning and leaping among the men and Makete, the two sons of Bubba eliminated ten of the assassins. In less than five minutes, all the attackers were dead.

"Holy lovin' shite boys. Ifin I knew ya could fight like that I wouldn't have been so worried these last months."

"We tried to tell you, Uncle Shea," John J. said.

"Yes. We were top of our class, uncle. In both academic and combat," Agni J. added.

"I can see why," Apolla said as she moved seductively toward the boys.

"Apolla," John laughed. "They're family."

"Emmm. Yeah, well, I'm not related to them."

"Listen here ya two strappin' horny fellas. Apolla here likes ta take trophy's, if ya know what I be sayin'. So think before ya do anythin' that might get yer privates hung on o' wall."

As Sheamus was explaining to John J. and his brother Agni, Apolla was checking the dead bodies for souvenirs. "Ugh, yeah, Uncle Shea. We get it."

"Alright. They know I'm coming. But I still want to do this on the down-low. My return is not going to become a spectacle. I have places we can go where the media and others won't bother us. So come on let's get the show on the road.

In an unused corn field outside the village, Sheamus and the boys saw John's ride. "What ta bleedin' hell, John," Sheamus said in awe.

"Yeah. It's an old Eagle Hell Fire. I fixed it up. Serves me well. Come on, we can all fit. My home is only about a hundred miles from here."

As John neared his cabin, Sheamus started to reorganize the terrain. Finally, as the Hell Fire flew over the last hill, Sheamus saw a familiar sight. On top of the biggest hill was the magnificent tree he and his father use to sit under when he was a boy. After landing and exiting from the chopper, Sheamus asked John, "How did ya happen ta pick this here spot? I know it weren't coincidence."

"No, it wasn't, Shea," John answered as he invited everyone into his cabin. "Remember when you told the story of you and your father under the tree to, Chara?" John said pointing up to the oak on the hill which was easily visible, even from John's cabin which sat a mile away.

"Well, I thought of that tree for years. When I left, I eventually found it. After decades of pain, war, noise and loss, I feel a sense of peace when I'm up there. I often sit under that oak and look out over these rolling green hills. From up there, the world seems clean, quite beautiful."

"Aye. That it does. Tis where me Da wanted to breathe his last."

"Everyone. Make yourself comfortable and Shea and I will be back in a bit," John said. Turning to Sheamus he asked, "Care to take a walk with me, *Uncle* Shea?" John smiled.

"Easy there, boyo'. Twasn't me who told them there boys to start that. Though...ugh..I'd have to admit I kind o' like it."

"I know the feeling. Ready to go up there?"

"Dropping his gear, Sheamus gave a wry smile and whispered, "Aye, Johnny boy….Aye."

When the two men arrived at the mammoth oak, they scanned the hills, admiring the beauty. Sitting down with their backs to the heavily barked tree Sheamus said, "Me Da loved this tree and these hills. He said it remanded him of ta Irish spirit. Solid, mighty no matter ta weather. He thought ta hills were like ta history o' Ireland. Ups and downs but rolling, not sharp. Most of all, this here tree was most like ta Irish people themselves, rooted deep in ta land, eternal."

"That it is, Shea. I love this place for many of the same reasons. I love this tree. Lots of strong deep roots, like the Roman family. Just as my family has looked out over the world all these centuries so does this tree look out over these hills. But my family, like this oak, can live without every root. I thought I had done all could. I thought it was time for others. I heard about Sam."

"Ya did? Then why not show up at the lad's funeral?"

"Why? Because the focus would have been on me. Because I was sick of funerals. Because I thought it wouldn't make a difference. Pick any or all of those."

"John! Ya can't just give up. What ta hell ya think Cass or Agni or our little Terry or Raiden would say? The fight ain't over till it's over. There's no pension plan for us. Carin' for this here world will most likely cost us our lives. But hell, John, tis what we were born inta. You've had o' life o' wealth and privilege. It comes with o' cost, laddybuck."

John pondered what Sheamus said and after a while he spoke, "Shea. I know you're right….It was the loss, the pain. It just built up over the years. The first was Terry. He trusted me and I couldn't keep him safe. Then Aimi, Raiden, Agni and many others. I failed to keep them alive. Don't you see? If I can't protect the people I love, how the hell can I protect the world? But the worst was Cass. I never wanted to outlive her. She was my world. She kept the pain away. After she died, I simply didn't care anymore. I'll admit it. I ran."

"Ok. Ya ran. Now what? Ya just gonna ignore everythin'? Time ta take o' stand, John. Get on yer feet and back ta savin' ta world or put o' bullet in yer brain right here."

John thought and then stood. "Yeah...Yeah." He then looked at the sun set behind the hills and said, "Fuck it. Let's go, my friend."

Chapter Thirteen

John Roman Returns

Back at the New Washington headquarters of the newly formed 'Humýsso' league, Tanach, Dan Kolla and Lenny Murtock were putting together their final plans for initiating a war with the Starlings.

"I feel the time is right, Murtock," Tanach said. "We have everything in place. All we have to do is push the button to start the show."

"Easy, Tanach. You have always been in such a hurry. This is a one time shot. If we fail, we'll all end up in prison or dead. There's no second chance," Murtock cautioned.

"I'm amazed how all you old fucks, with so little time left to live, always want to go slow. You and your pals in the Senate have been working on this for how many years, ten, twenty? I'm sick of waiting. We have people in the military who will implement the moon and Mars sabotage. We have people here in the police and political arena who will back our play. When do we go? After the Starlings die of old age?" Tanach yelled as she drank down more whiskey.

"I'm kind of with Tanach on this, Lenny. What do you think a good time would be?" Dan Kolla asked.

"You're right, Tanach. We have been planning this for years. Some of us are much older than you and Dan. But it's that experience, that patience which will prevail in the end. We're talking about the overthrow of a government and simultaneously changing the mind sets of a majority of humans and Anaptýsso. For us to be successful, we cannot have one without the other. All of that takes planning, patience, and time. We are almost there, and if you need a definite day or hour I'd say a year," Lenny answered.

"A YEAR!!!" Tanach exploded. Moving to Murtock, Tanach put her knife to his throat.

"Hear me, you motherfucker. If you and the rest of your fossilized buddies think me and my people are going to wait another year, you're fucking crazy. I've listened to that, 'next year' bullshit for too long. I want to move on the Starlings and the opposition by the end of the week. You understand?" Pressing the knife into Lenny's neck Tanach said, "Tell me you understand." Murtock slowly nodded his head yes. "Good. Good. Because if you don't I will begin without you and your friends. Then, when we win, I will execute anyone who didn't help."

Tanach removed her knife from Murtock's neck and as he rubbed his throat he looked at Tanach with hate and fear. "Alright. Alright. If you insist. I'll tell everyone to begin the process. But even if you slice my head off, we can't possibly be ready in just a week. Give me until the end of the month. I must coordinate, not just the

Nations but our affiliates on the moon and Mars. Let's say June 1st. That will be the beginning of, 'Operation Cleansing'," Murtock pledged.

Tanach looked at Lenny, her eyes piercing into him, her face and body manic. As she paced back and forth, Murtock didn't know if she would agree or kill him. Finally stopping, she took a deep breath and said, "Ok….Ok." Coming within an inch of Murtock's face and letting the blade of her knife caress his face Tanach continued, "I'll wait until the first. No longer. Don't fail us Lenny. You won't like me if you fail me. Understand?"

Slowly pulling her knife from his face Lenny whispered, "Yes, Tanach. I understand."

"Good. Tell me what the plan is."

"Alright. On the technically, legal front, Senator Zano will introduce the 'Fairness in Access' bill. It's just a pile of mumbo jumbo but in-between the lines it gives the UGN control over the moon and Mars. By that I mean any installations, discoveries, governing will all be in the hands of the UGN. Starlings will have no say in anything concerning the moon or Mars. Senators Masoto and Collins will second the bill. Now, and I caution you not to…oh..how shall I put this? Overreact. Despite your passion for what we are going to do, not everyone is on board. We were hoping for more *time* but you have made your position on that subject clear," Murtock sighed.

"Yeah, I have. So stop the bellyaching and continue," Tanach said, clearly irritated.

"Yeah. Come on. Tell us what's next," Dan chirped in.

"Shut the fuck up, Kolla. You're only here because of your father," Tanach responded.

"What!!. I fought John Roman in Rus. Was tortured in his prison, and never cracked I might add. Then I...." Tanach grabbed Dan by the collar and said, "Yeah and you failed on both counts asshole. You lost in Rus and you spilled the beans without even knowing you did. Look. I fucked you a couple of times because I needed a dick that day. You also make me laugh once in a while but you have no say in any of this. Stand back, follow my orders, and have that dick ready when I need it. Do that and I might let you stick around. Now shut up and let the adults talk."

Tanach let go and Dan sat down with the look of a chastised boy. Turning to Lenny she said, "Continue."

"Ehh, yes..well. We know we have close to the votes needed to pass the resolution, but we can't guarantee it will pass. We desperately need three senators to join us, but they are on the fence."

"Do you have the list of those needing convincing?"

"Why, yes." Murtock snapped his fingers and a beautiful young woman produced the list he wanted.

"Here, my dear. If you can convince these three, Senators, Hope, Lang and Tallow, then the resolution will pass."

Taking the information, Tanach then said, "Ok. Then what?"

"Then what, what?" Murtock asked.

"After the resolution passes, you fucking idiot," Tanach yelled.

Murtock looked down at the floor and then slowly raised his head. Then in a calm but forceful voice said, "You know, Tanach, I am one of the most powerful, most wealthy people on earth. I have joined you in this endeavor, because I do think the Starlings would eventually not need nor want us. That could lead to our decline or even elimination. But I will not have you yell, threaten me or demand things from me like some petulant child. If you continue this behavior, I'm out." Suddenly, twenty fully-armed men entered the room. "These are my friends," Lenny said, pointing to the menacing group of men.

Tanach realized she had pushed Murtock too far. Though she said to herself, 'I'll kill this old fuck later,' she knew flattery should be her weapon now. In a flash, Tanach became a sultry sexy kitten. She moved across the room as all eyes watched her transformation. Standing next to Murtock she purred, "Lenny….Lenny." As she stroked his face and lips with one hand while caressing his crotch with the other. "You...know...me. I'm high-spirited. You didn't seem to mind it when I was fucking you. Look, I know you're right. I'm sorry about the knife thing. It's just because you make me so hot when you're forceful. Please forgive me. We still are going to kick this plan off on the first….right...Lenny," Tanach cooed as she drove her tongue into his ear.

Aroused, his anger softened, Murtock said, "Ye...Yes...Tanach. Maybe you were right. I would say we have been inert these last few years and yes, you have convinced me it's time. However, we must get those three senators to our side. Can you do that?"

"Lenny, honey. I got you hard at your age. I can do anything. You'll have those votes by the weekend. So after the law is passed then what?"

Composing himself Murtock continued, "Yes. Ahh….a week after the vote, some attacks on cities and the moon will be blamed on the Starlings. Our media will blanket the internet, airwaves, and print with anti-Starling propaganda. Then, when enough anger and fear has been integrated into the public consciousness we will unleash a virus on the moon and Mars. After the world's battle with viruses no one will want to get involved with saving the Starlings. The populace will think it's what the Starlings deserve. Our media will make sure of that. Within a year, all the Starlings will be dead. The earth, moon and Mars will be ours again."

Tanach smiled and thought to herself, "Yeah, then we can start thinking about getting rid of these fucking red monsters."

****

When John and Sheamus, along with Apolla and the boys returned to Tsalaki they did so in secret. Together, they and Terry, who had been released on bond, rendezvoused at a location known only to a select group of people.

"I want to thank you for getting me out, John. Don't know how you did it, but thanks." Terry said.

"When I left, I put in place certain safety protocols. I have many friends who I keep secret. They had orders for such problems. Most of those orders were to help protect Sam, but they also extended to you, Bubba etc," John answered.

"Yeah. About Bubba," Terry sighed.

"What ta fuck happened, Terry," Sheamus asked.

"I have found out since my release, that Bubba went to see Archieréas. I told him where a set of f-drives were which contained all the names of the traitors. Apparently, Archieréas had his own traitors. After giving him the f-drives, Tanach Roman…"

"Don't call her Roman," John said.

"Sure, John. Tanach took everyone hostage, grabbed the f-drives, and killed Archieréas. Bubba escaped but all the running at his age…his heart gave out. I'm sorry, John. It's my fault for getting him into this at his age. I should have…"

"Should have what, Terry? Waited? For who? If anyone is to blame it's me. I'm the one who ran off. Where's Kimiko? Where's Bubba's body? What about Archieréas?"

"Bubba told me he was going to send Kimiko's to Uli wa Liánhé. The Anaptýsso took Archieréas. I don't know where. The new high priest for the Anaptýsso is named 'Sacerdos'. He is vehemently pro-Starling. Bubba is still at the morgue. His body is unclaimed. I think the anti-Starling faction is using his body to lure Kimiko out. A resolution called the 'Fairness in Access' bill, will be voted on the first of June. It's a load of crap. It's supposed to give everyone access to the moon, Mars and a bunch of other bullshit. The real purpose is to disenfranchise the Starlings."

"Alright. That means we have one week. Shea. I want you to go to Uli wa Liánhé. See Akemi Kameyama. She's Raiden's sister and is running the family now. John, Agni. I want you to keep tabs on Tanach and her followers. But don't, under any circumstances, confront her or her people. You understand?"

"Yes, John. Just observe. We got it," John J. answered.

"I disagree, stud," Apolla interjected.

"Why?" John asked.

"Listen lover. You may be good in bed but you know nothing about how women think. She'll spot these two a mile away and eat them for breakfast. Tanach doesn't know me. I'm the one who can get close enough to her that it matters."

John looked at Apolla and then John and Agni, J. "Yes. You're right. You go."

"What are we going to do?" Agni asked.

"We left our father against his wishes. We may have got him killed. If any of you think we are just going to sit around while...." John put his hands on both boy's shoulders.

"John. Agni. You did *not* get your father killed. Don't ever think that. Bubba was the bravest most honorable man I knew. He did what he had to. It was Tanach, Murtock, Dan Kolla and all the other traitors who led to his death. First, we're going to put your dad to rest. Then you two are going to be my body guards. Whatever happens, we'll be in this together. Understand. You both are *Lads* now. Right, Shea."

"Aye, John. That makes us five again. Unless….ehhh," Sheamus turned to Apolla. "you wantin' ta be o' member there, darlin'."

"Dream on, you old fart. The last thing this lady needs is to be in a boy's club. I'll pass. Besides I am here for John and John only. I could give a shit who runs things out here. I'm am and always will be an Outlander."

"Well, I guess that settles that laddie bucks. Tis we five now. Put yer hands out there now, Lads."

Terry, John Sheamus and John and Agni J. all put their hands out simultaneously as they stood in a circle. As their hands all touched they chanted in unison. "We are the Lads. Forever, *Custodes Mundi!!*"

Chapter Fourteen

The Final Battle

The next day at Bubba's service, his sons, Terry, Sheamus and John spoke as they passed the urn holding Bubba's ashes among them.

"We loved our Dad. He taught us to be honest, honorable, kind and courageous. We are proud to follow in his footsteps," John J, said as he passed the urn.

"Our Dad was the best father any son could hope for. He could be tough on us but it was always with love and our best interests at heart. We love you Dad. We hope one day that you, mom and John and me will be reunited," Agni J. said as he wiped his tears.

"I knew you for twenty years my friend. My uncle Terry thought the world of you and so did I. There was never a time you weren't friendly, or smiling that big grin of yours.' I'll miss you Bubba. Not just for awhile bit for the rest of my life," Terry said passing the urn.

"We had our differences, Bubba me lad, but you'll always be me brother, ya big bloody gallopin' beautiful bastard ya. Rest now, me friend. Rest."

Holding Bubba's urn, John was last to speak, "I met you on the first days of this journey my friend. We've traveled a lot of miles together since then. I have a few more to go, but I know you'll be with me. You left a loving wife and two beautiful sons. That's a lot more than most can claim. You were one of a kind Bubba. Wherever you are I'm sure people are glad you're there. I'm already jealous of them. I'll watch over Kimiko and the boys. That I promise."

After all the speeches John was approached by Lenny Murtock. Accompanied by several senators and a few military personnel, Lenny said, "I see the great John Roman has returned. I hope you don't plan on stirring up any trouble, John."

"It's Mister Roman to you, Murtock," John replied as he moved to within inches of Murtock's face. "What I plan to do, or not to do, is none of your business. I'm here for my friend's funeral. If you have a problem with that I could give two fucks."

Two of the military men moved toward John. All four of the other Lads started moving also but Lenny stopped his people. "Now, now Mr. Roman. I want no trouble with you or your friends. I'm a live and let live kind of guy. I'm not even angry about you tossing me in prison. So how about telling these comrades of yours to cool down."

"We're at Bubba Johnson's funeral. Those are his sons. We were his dear friends. I hold you and your cohorts responsible. So, no. we won't cool down," John said with his temper rising.

"Fine. Fine, Mr. Roman. We'll leave before you try to have me arrested on trumped up charges like last time. Even though I don't think you have that kind of power anymore," Murtock said as he pointed to the police who were clearly on Lenny's payroll. "Change is coming Mr. Roman. Join us or get out of the way. Otherwise you all may end up like your friend here."

After Murtock and his people left, Bubba's two sons were handed his ashes. "You two need to go with Shea. See your mother. Then come back."

John and Agni couldn't contain their tears as they held their fathers urn. "Thank you, John," both boys said in unison. John took Sheamus to the side and whispered, "Shea. Get to Uli wa Liánhé. Pay our respects to Kimiko, then get those f-drives from her and your asses back here by tomorrow. Got it?"

"Ya can count on me boyo'." John then went to the boys and placed a kiss on Bubba's urn. "I'll see you on the other side, my friend."

****

The next day, Sheamus and Bubba's sons met Kimiko at Akemi Kameyama's compound. John and Agni ran to their mother and after all the hugs and kisses, they presented their father's ashes to her. "I am so glad you both are safe. But I'm sure you will not stay, will you?" Kimiko asked.

"No, mother. We must help finish what father was trying to," Agni said.

"I understand. I don't like it but I understand. Shea, please look after my boys."

"I will, Kimiko. I've traveled with them for months now. They are capable strong men. Hell it be them who will most likely be lookin' after this here old Irish fart."

"Here are the f-drives. I made copies and gave them to Akemi. She has assured me of their safe keeping," Kimiko said.

"Can ya trust ta gentlewoman ta keep them hidden?" Akemi entered the room and answered, "I assure you, Mr. O'Keefe, the f-drive copies are most safe. John loved my sister, Aimi and was a friend to my brother, Raiden. So for that alone, I am honor bound to protect Kimiko, you and the drives. I also share your ideas for this world, so you can trust I am on your side,"

Sheamus bowed to Akemi and replied, "I meant no offense yer ladyship. It's just that lately o' whole lot o' people have been turnin' traitor. It sort o' puts o' man in o' paranoid state, ya might say."

"I understand, Mr. O'Keefe. No offense taken," Akemi said.

"Fine. But please, just Shea. I not be one ta hold titles or such."

"As you wish, Shea. I would suggest you leave Kimiko here. She will be safe. These people you are going against like to take hostages and hurt loved ones. There have already been some threats to my family but nothing my people can't handle. And please, just, Akemi."

"Very well then, Akemi. Hope we meet again under less stressful circumstances," Sheamus said as he and the boys left.

****

A day later everyone was back in Tsalaki. In one of John's safe houses, John met with the two Starlings who were going to speak at the UGN. "John Roman. I cannot tell you how happy my son and I are to meet you. I am Invictus R. Moonchild, and this is my son Astrum," Invictus said as he shook John's hand.

"Bleedin' hell. Ifin all three of ya don't look ta spittin' image," Sheamus said.

"I'm sure we do, Mr. O'Keefe. But *we* most certainly can tell the differences between our kind." Astrum said.

"Yes. Eventually more changes will happen over generations. But for now, looking like the father of our kind is something we're proud of," Invictus responded.

"Hey. I'm not the father of anyone. I just donated some blood and cells and Cass and the other scientists did the rest."

"It was still your cells, your blood, John. I'm afraid you can't stop us from being grateful. You're just going to have to suffer our admiration," Invictus said with a smile.

John chuckled and said, "Alright. Ok. But please just don't start reciting prayers or anything like that."

"Don't worry, John. Starlings are atheistic. We admire, we don't worship," Invictus said.

John smiled, "That sounds good. So, Invictus. Where do the Starlings stand? You must know this whole set-up is being done by a small group of people. They have used lies, media, bribes and threats to get us where we are. The majority of humans and Anaptýsso are good, peaceful individuals."

"We agree, John. We have no desire to hurt humans or Anaptýsso. We look at them and see our grandmothers and grandfathers. We have no intentions of doing any harm. In fact, we come with nothing but good news."

Invictus then showed John and the rest of the group what he and his son had brought.

"Reveal this to everyone at the UGN and I'm sure you'll change a lot of minds, Invictus," John said.

"We think so. Our only concern is that we are able to do so without interruption or attack," Invictus replied.

"Don't ya worry, yer lordship. Ta Lads will make sure ya get ta say what ya needs ta."

"He's right, Invictus. We'll be there. You and your son will be safe. You have my word," John pledged.

"Then that's all we need." Invictus bowed with his hand over his heart, "May you live long among the stars, John Roman."

****

On the first, every senator, news outlet, many military personnel, national observers, a crowd of everyday people and Anaptýsso filled the galleries and floor of the UGN consortium's annual meeting. Everyone knew the 'Fairness in Access' bill was going to be voted on. Groups from both sides gathered, many carrying slogans and chanting their positions. On the floor before the bill vote, Invictus R. Moonchild was asked to speak. He and his son Astrum R. Moonchild had come to earth for this important moment. In the halls behind the speaker's podium were Tanach and Lenny Murtock.

"Have we got the votes?" Tanach asked Lenny.

"It's going to be close. Did you secure the three senators I needed?"

"Of course. Lang took the money. Collins had good taste."

"What does that mean?"

"She liked the taste of my pussy." Murtock looked at Tanach.

"Hey. You think this shit," Tanach said proudly as she pointed to her body, "only works on men?"

"What about Tallow?"

"Yeah. He's a little tied up at the moment." Lenny seemed shocked, but Tanach assured him Tallow was ok.

"Don't fret, Lenny. When Tallow awakes, he won't remember a thing. Hey, a vote that's not against us is as good as one for us right?"

Murtock composed himself. "We'll see. One thing in this world anyone can count on is a politician lying. On paper we have the votes, but one never knows until the tally."

"I'll not be thwarted by lying politicians, Lenny. If this thing doesn't go our way legally, I've those with me who will make it happen my way."

"I won't be part of that kind of thing."

"Suit yourself, Lenny. I guess you better hope the vote goes our way then. Otherwise, you'll be part of the problem like them."

"Is that a threat?"

"No, Lenny," Tanach purred as she stroked Murtock's crotch, "It's a promise."

"Ladies and Gentlemen. Honored guests and those in the gallery, welcome to the United Global Nations annual meeting. There was a chorus of shouts and applause. Senator Zano pounded his gavel. "We have decided to take up the 'Fairness in Access' bill as our first action in this meeting. But before we do, Senator Thomas Franklin has invited Invictus R. Moonchild and his son Astrum to speak to this august body." Immediately there was an equal pandemonium of both boos and affirmations.

"Order!! Order!!" Zano shouted as he banged his gavel on the desk. "May I remind the body that it is the right of any senator to call a guest when a bill is presented for vote. Now, please sit and let's all hear what Senator Franklin and his guests have to say. We will then vote."

At the podium, Franklin was again met with both boos and ayes. "My fellow Earthers. What we have before us is a bill, the so-called 'Fairness in Access' which could mean the end of all of us."

Boos and yells of approval rained down, and again Zano had to bang his gavel.

"So all of you can get a clear idea of what this bill would mean, I have invited Invictus R. Moonchild and his son Astrum. Please listen to what they have to say and then vote your conscience."

The room became filled with a deafening roar, and a few fights broke out, Invictus stood at the podium, patiently waiting for calm. After ten minutes of his standing solemnly, the room went silent.

"My fellow citizens of the Earth, moon and Mars, I, Invictus R. Moonchild, a Starling, has brought you gifts. Many on earth think we Starlings want to do humans and Anaptýsso harm. Nothing could be further from the truth. To us, humans and Anaptýsso are like our fathers and mothers. We would not exist if it weren't for both of you. We honor you in our teachings. We respect you in our culture. We admire your resilience, your adventurous spirit, your compassion and honor. We could no more hurt you than we could our children. Here at my side is my son who can tell you that in our schools, our children are taught to think of humans and Anaptýsso with respect; to admire and honor them.

Some say we are leaving you behind. That we are keeping the riches of the universe from you. Again, nothing could be further from the truth. Here, let me show you." Invictus then removed his outer cloak. "This vest you see me wearing is an anti-gravity vest, made by a combination of rare elements not found on earth, and our technology. With this vest, I can stand here and not be bothered by earth's gravity." The crowd was astounded as Invictus danced a little bit around the podium. "The best part is this vest works both ways. Humans can now go to the moon and Mars and not be affected by the gravity. For the Anaptýsso, we have this." Invictus held up a small vial. "This contains nanobots. Again made possible by our mining of Mars and asteroids. These rare elements make the nanobots possible. Injecting these into an Anaptýsso, prevents the background noise from the Big-Bang injuring their senses thus freeing the Anaptýsso from the confines of earth." The room erupted in, "Ohhs" and "hurrahs". After it quieted, Invictus spoke, "These are just some of the marvels we have for you. You see, we don't want to keep these wonders from you; we want to share them with you. We want all of you to join us in this great adventure of exploring the universe. It is only together that *all* our hopes and dreams will come true. There are wonders and marvels that will take thousands of years to unfold. Only together can we face the future of such unknown miracles. Please join us, and together we will spread across the galaxy and beyond as one united people."

The room burst into applause and shouts of "Starlings," "Starlings." Many of the anti-Starling supporters threw down their signs and joined the pro-Starling side. Some of the anti-Starling group left in disgust but their numbers were few. John, Sheamus and Apolla were clapping and smiling. Terry was in the balcony watching for any trouble but got caught up in the celebration. Bubba's sons were trying to get near Invictus but the crowd was packed shoulder to shoulder. John looked at the crowd and got worried, "Shea. I don't like the looks of this. Too many getting too close to Invictus," John shouted over the din.

"I hear ya, mate. I'll fight me way through to ta other side. Take yerself ta the right."

"Apolla. See if anyone is behind the stage. Take some men with you," John said as he stared toward Invictus.

"Fuck that. A man's good for one thing and that's fucking. Most times, he's not even good for that," Apolla laughed as she headed back stage.

"Well, that's that," Murtock said as he signaled his men to move out. Tanach grabbed him by his collar and spun him around. "What the fuck you mean, that's that? I told you today is it. We make our move TODAY!!" Lenny removed Tanach's hand and his men took hold of her. Murtock then slapped Tanach across the face several times.

"You fucking bitch!! I told you to wait. I said we weren't ready. We could have pulled this off but, NO!! You couldn't wait. Well lets see how you handle my boys. You're done Tanach. After my men get through fucking the shit out of you they're going to toss your body ov…" Murtock didn't finish his statement because Dan

Kola's head rolled across his foot. He looked up in time to see all his men being killed by Makete. Two of the red warriors grabbed Murtock. Tanach slowly walk to him and said, "You think I'm an idiot. Some little girl you can fuck and then throw away?" Tanach undid Lenny's pants and in a flash cut off his balls and dick with the Starling ceremonial knife. One of the Makete held Murtock's mouth closed so he couldn't scream. Tanach held up Lenny's manhood and showed it to him. "I'm going to do that to that Starling fuck and then to the whole Roman family. Open his mouth," She ordered the Makete. As soon as Murtock's mouth was pried apart, Tanach shoved the man's dick and balls down his throat.

Apolla saw what happened and said, "I like to stuff them and reuse them. Otherwise it's a waste of an entirely good cock. Though by looking at the size of that one I'd say you did the right thing."

"Who the fuck are you?" Tanach asked.

"Oh just a little ole gal who is going to kill you," Apolla laughed as she leapt toward Tanach. Coming down, Apolla ran her knife across Tanach's ribs. It would have been a kill except a Makete had grabbed Apolla's foot and pulled her back. Looking at her wound, Tanach yelled, "Kill her." As Apolla became busy with fighting the Makete, Tanach ran toward Invictus ready to plunge her knife into his back.

John heard the noise coming from behind the stage and quickly signaled Sheamus and the boys. Bulldozing his way to Invictus he saw three men about to attack Astrum, but John J. and Agni J. got in their way. Time seemed to slow as John saw Tanach jumping toward Invictus with her knife coming down. John leaped onto Invictus' back and felt Tanach's knife plunge into him. Pulling out her knife Tanach yelled, "Die, you Roman dog."

Before she could finish John, she froze. Standing there looking at John with more hate than any one person should have, Tanach began to fall to the floor. Sheamus had thrown his switchblade and sent it through the back of Tanach's neck. Apolla came out from behind the stage, having done away with the Morphs. She was bloodied but would recover. She knelt by John, who was on the floor being held by Invictus, and said, "You don't look so good."

"I'll be alright. These fucks couldn't fight a kitten. Looks like you had some fun though," Apolla said, as she inspected John's wound.

As Sheamus and the boys were ensuring everyone was safe, John said to Apolla, "Where are you going from here?"

"That bad huh?" Apolla asked.

"Yeah. Seems so," John replied.

"Well my *Lyubovnik*," Apolla whispered. "Back to the Outlands for this girl. It's where I'll end my days. You know I love you, right?"

"Never doubted it," John smiled.

Apolla never said anything to anyone else. She just turned, wiped a tear from her face and left.

"John. You must let us take you to the hospital," Invictus said.

"No. I'll be fine. I'm glad I met you, Invictus, and your son. Keep your word. The things you said here today. Keep y....you...your word."

"We most certainly will, John Roman. You are the *all-father*. We could never lie to you. We thank you for making us,"

"Yeah well. You should thank Cass for that. Just take care of everyone. My family has a motto, (cough)."

"Yes the Starlings know it well," Astrum said.

"Change it. *Nos sumus custodes*. It's more suited now."

"We will, John Roman."

"Alright. Alright. Stand aside now yer takin' up ta man's oxygen," Sheamus said.

Kneeling by John Sheamus whispered, "How yer feelin' laddie buck?"

"Get me out of here, my friend." Sheamus tore the robe Invictus had been wearing and wrapped it around John's wound. Lifting him up he started walking him out of the Institute. John nodded for the boys and Terry to follow. All five ended at John's Eagle Hell Fire. "Terry. I need you to fly me and Shea to the cabin in Ireland. John, Agni, come here."

The boys approached John with a little trepidation. "Yes, sir."

"Listen to me. You men are the future of the Roman Institute. I've left instructions for Terry and Shea. If you want, I have set up an adoption for the both of you. You will become John Johnson Roman and Agni Johnson Roman."

"Yes, John. We would like that very much."

"Good. Good. Now go and help the people who were at the UGN meeting. Terry will help you with the other stuff when he gets back. Make me and your dad proud."

As Sheamus strapped John into the bird he started to breath heavily.

"Come on Terry, me lad. Hurry it up," Sheamus said.

"We'll get there Shea. I'm going to put in overdrive."

Two hours later, they landed. As Sheamus helped John out of the Eagle, John shook Terry's hand. "Get back to the Institute. I'm counting on you and Shea to help those boys."

"You have my word, John." As the copter rose and flew away John said to Sheamus, "I Think I'm going to need a hand to get there, brother."

"Don't worry about o' thin' Johnny boy. Ya can count on Sheamus O'Keefe, me lad."

Thirty minutes later they were on top of the hill where Sheamus and his father spent many a sunset. Sheamus sat John down at the foot of the ancient massive oak tree. There John let out a long winded breath. "Ohh, Shea. It feels good just to sit. No worries, no demands, no loss, no pain. I'm so tired Shea. I've lost so many. They come to me in my dreams."

Leaning against the tree as he did with his father, Sheamus said, "Aye, lad. Them there's ta ghosts. They love ya and want ya ta be with them. I dream them too."

"I understand why your father...(cough) came here. Look at that sunset, Shea. An ocean of rolling green hills. Have you...(cough) ever seen anything so beautiful?"

"Nay, brother. No where else on this here earth but mother Ireland herself."

"Did we (cough) did we make a difference, Shea?"

"Ya damn right we did, lad."

"Good...Good. (cough). I think...I'll close...my eyes for a bit."

Standing against the tree, with his hand on John's shoulder and a tear in his eye; Sheamus silently watched the sun set.

Made in the USA
Columbia, SC
13 February 2021